*The Cape Cod National Seashore is the setting for **THE LITTLE STRIKER,** which tells the story of TARA, a Least Tern. It is a nature story and the author relates a sensitive and perceptive insight into what he feels man's relationship with his environment should be.*

***THE LITTLE STRIKER** is a poignant, eloquent story of TARA's endless struggle for survival. Few readers will remain unaffected by TARA or her quest.*

The photographs are not intended to distract the reader from the Author's descriptions in the story. Their use is simply to add another dimension to those who are unfamiliar with the natural beauty of the area.

THE LITTLE STRIKER

A Cape Cod Nature Story
Set in the Cape Cod National Seashore

By Russell G. Moore

Library of Congress Catalog Card Number 81-80507

ISBN 0-936972-03-3

FIRST EDITION

Published by:

Lower Cape Publishing, P.O. Box 901, Orleans, Mass. 02653

For the Children:

Christine

Cynthia

Clay

"THERE GREW SLOWLY IN ME AN UNSPEAKABLE CONVICTION THAT WE HAVE NO RIGHT TO INFLICT SUFFERING AND DEATH ON ANOTHER LIVING CREATURE UNLESS THERE IS SOME UNAVOIDABLE NECESSITY FOR IT, AND THAT WE OUGHT ALL OF US TO FEEL WHAT A HORRIBLE THING IT IS TO CAUSE SUFFERING AND DEATH OUT OF MERE THOUGHTLESSNESS."

ALBERT SCHWEITZER

AUTHOR'S NOTE

The Little Striker is, of course, fiction, and except for the Great Blizzard of 1978, the events that take place on Cape Cod, and in Tara's life, exist only in the author's imagination. In addition, the author accepts total responsibility for any scientific liberties he has taken to enhance the story.

The Least Tern is considered to be on the endangered species list in California, and it is the author's opinion that the sequence of events which occur in *The Little Striker* can take place in the future on Cape Cod. We must all remind ourselves that the extinction of any species of flora, fauna or avifauna can and will occur if cooperative efforts are not taken to protect natural habitats.

In regards to the Least Tern, what I hope for is that *The Little Striker* makes more people aware of their plight, that it makes more people more concerned for their future, and that it motivates more people to call for more protective measures.

So, by adding Tara's voice to those which have gone before, I hope that this beautiful and innocent piece of life can be persuaded to stay with us as long as we have a Cape Cod.

RGM

DECEMBER 1980

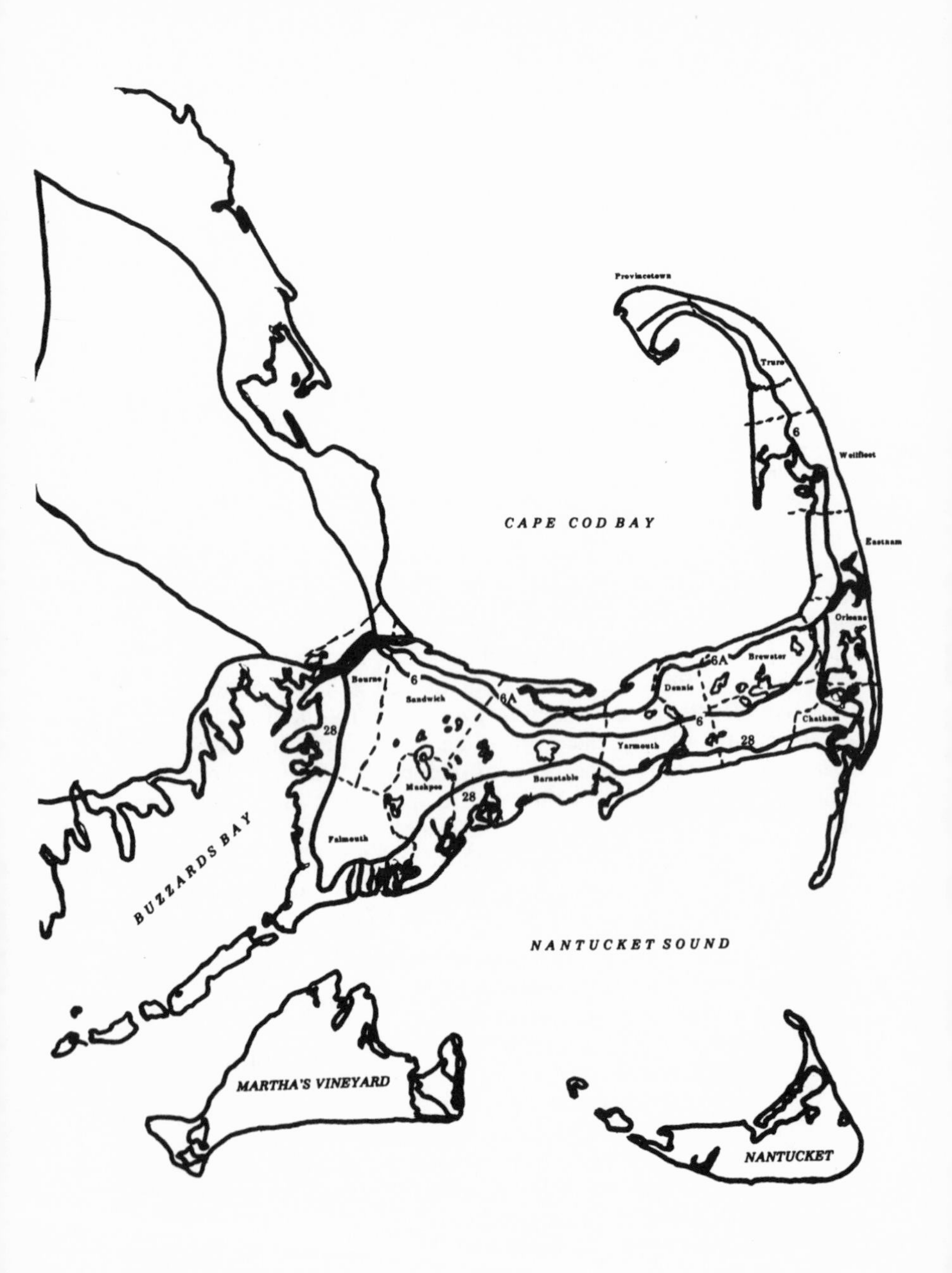

Cape Cod and the Islands

PROLOGUE

There were many things that Tara would never know . . . or understand.

She would never know that she was a vertebrate, or more accurately, a bird of the Class *Aves*. The Class consists of twenty-seven Orders and Tara belonged to the Order reserved for shorebirds, gulls and alcids . . . *Charadriiformes*. Her Family name was *Laridae* which included the gulls and terns, and below this was the Subfamily *Sterninae* which was reserved for over fifty Species of terns, ten of which called North America their breeding home. She was of the Genus *Sterna* which includes the Species of *paradisaea,* the Arctic Tern; *hirundo,* the Common Tern; *dougallii,* the Roseate Tern; and *fosteri,* the Foster's Tern. Tara, however, was none of these. She was a *Sterna Albifrons,* the Least Tern, one of the smaller Species of her Genus. But, she did not know this.

It had been ten thousand years before her birth when the sands of Cape Cod had had their beginning. The glacier had finally melted, the climate of the Northern Hemisphere had warmed and the waters of the North Atlantic had poured across the plains of Cape Cod Bay and Nantucket Sound. The enlarging ocean had isolated the two islands later to be called Nantucket and Martha's Vineyard, and had washed against the virgin peninsula to the north which jutted out from the North American mainland. The Cape had not existed before the coming of the glacier, but rather had been a monumental gift from the north, and had been carried southward beneath the unimaginable and relentless power of the ten thousand foot thick cap of ice.

Then, the wind and water had taken command. In the beginning, all that had existed had been a primeval scythe of glacial till whose rough and hoary shore had been indented with coarse bays and untouched headlands, and where nothing had lived upon its cold and barren earth.

Year after year had passed, and season had followed season. In summers, the wind had alternated, blowing either from the southeast or the southwest, at first pushing the waves against the towering scarp of the Great Outer Beach, then towards the smaller seacliffs bordering Nantucket Sound and the bay coast. These forces of nature had been gentle but persistent while their warmth had disguised their strength and endurance as they chewed away at the scarp.

In addition, while centuries of winters had followed centuries of winters, the icy winds had streamed across the cold waters of the Atlantic and had propelled the massive storm waves towards the fragile shore with a fierce intensity. Gradually, the scarp had retreated at a rate of three feet each year. The hungry waters had claimed fifty-four thousand cubic yards of till from each mile of scarp and it had made little difference what the temper of the waves had been. Relentlessly, they had continued their assault down through the years.

Whether being driven by nasty, numbing northeasters, or by horrifying, tropical hurricanes; whether being caressed deceptively by gentle southwest breezes, or being lashed by northwest gales of fast moving Arctic cold fronts, the waves had continued their persistent sculpturing and smoothing of the defenseless scarp.

And thus the barrier beaches had been born. The Provincelands, Sandy Neck, Nauset Beach, North Beach, Monomoy, and many others. All had once been the glacial till of the scarp. Once the till had been returned to the sea, the longshore currents had moved it north and south, east and west. Where the coast had curved inward, the sand had refused to follow, but instead had continued straight ahead. Shoals had formed first, and then these had given way to sandbars. When at last the tides had been unable to flow across these bars, the barrier beaches had been shaped, and behind these, the salt marshes.

Tara could never know the history of her ancestors. She could never know that hundreds of years ago, her species had bred and multiplied along the coast of southern California, the Gulf coast from Texas eastward, southward across the Bahamas to the West Indies, British Honduras and Venezuela, and the east coast from Florida to Cape Cod.

She was also unaware that her ancestors had discovered and colonized the Cape Cod island beaches and had been a part of their history for centuries. Her great-great-grandparents had originated the family colony at the tip of Coast Guard Beach in the early nineteen hundreds and the family tree had continued in existence there until the present time.

For hundreds of years the terns of Cape Cod had led their precious, innocent lives in rhythm to the changing seasons. Twice

Cape Cod, outer beach

each year they had migrated up and down the east coast of the United States as they had responded to the earth's yearly journey around the sun.

The Arctic Terns had barely glanced at the New England coast on their way northward. A few of the lazier ones, however, had chosen not to nest in the land of the midnight sun, and instead had reared their young along the coasts of Greenland, Nova Scotia, Maine and Cape Cod. In late summer, on their return journey to the Antarctic, many of them had paused briefly on the outer beaches of the Cape before flying eastward to the western shores of Europe.

Meanwhile, the Common Tern had frolicked alongside the Least Tern, and together the two species, along with the less frequent Roseate Tern, had glorified the Cape Cod beaches from Buzzard's Bay to Provincetown.

These four species were the sea-swallows, the mackerel gulls, the paradise terns, or the little strikers. They were called many names depending on who was naming them, and why. Actually, these terns were seabirds and close relatives of the gulls. They were small to medium in size, slender and long-winged, often with deeply forked tails. Rarely did they rest upon the water, and their small webbed feet were good reason why they did not swim well. Their body structure, however, was well developed and highly specialized for exquisite flying and their long, tapering wings carried their bodies effortlessly in light, airy flights as they bounded over the hot, sandy beaches.

Then, one hundred years before her birth, Tara's great-great-great-grandparents had been flying over a Monomoy salt marsh when they had been shot down along with tens of thousands of other sea and shore birds. This had been the time when their feathers had been highly coveted as plumes by the burgeoning millinery trade, and was the beginning of countless atrocities committed against them. Many species had been almost destroyed. But finally, laws had been passed protecting them and the other avifauna, and gradually the meager populations had recovered during the early part of the twentieth century.

But even so, each spring and summer during the nesting season, they had been preyed upon by many natural enemies. When gulls had moved into the colonies of those Least Terns nesting on island beaches, they had reluctantly joined those nesting on the barrier beaches. Here, they had been vulnerable to the onslaught of crows, owls, weasels and skunks. But they had coped with these predators just as they had struggled against the flood and storm tides that had overflowed their nests and had drowned their chicks.

Following the turn of the century, increased availability of the railroad train and the automobile had opened the Cape to a greater

Common Terns

influx of tourists and vacationers, and through the years the natural environment had been gradually changed to accommodate this new source of revenue. This commercialization of the Cape had proceeded at a leisurely pace until the end of World War Two, but following this period until the time of Tara's birth in nineteen hundred and seventy-three, little concern had been shown for the Cape as an ecosystem.

There had been a few exceptions. One was the Cape Cod National Seashore which had been signed into law by John Kennedy, and now its twenty-seven thousand acres sprawled across the Lower Cape from Chatham to Provincetown. But even here, where thousands of terns had prospered for hundreds of years, they had been pushed into a miserable, struggling existence, and were now slowly expiring ignobly in the cause of "civilization."

Because of this combination of natural predation and unnatural human encroachment, the populations of the terns in general and the Least Tern in particular had been declining steadily since the nineteen twenties. The gradual abandonment of their traditional Cape Cod nesting sites was the result of the actions of the ignorant, the self-serving, and the unconcerned.

During Tara's lifetime, the nesting sites had been rapidly disappearing beneath the wheels of the dunebuggies, the careless trampling of the tourists, and the hungry predators. Monomoy, the island of the shifting sands, had been one of the first areas to be abandoned when the exploding herring gull population had taken over the nesting sites of the Least Tern. In the meantime, similar occurrences had taken place on the chain of the Elizabeth Islands, the entire U-shaped coast of Buzzard's Bay, and the Massachusetts coast from the Canal to Boston.

Yes, the nineteen seventies and early nineteen eighties had been excruciatingly dismal and frustrating for her. The nesting sites had slowly disappeared at Corn Hill, Indian Neck, West Dennis, Craigville, Osterville, Waquoit, Sandy Neck and Tern Island. All had fallen away as the concept of environmental protection had been ignored during the late nineteen seventies when the indifferent towns had failed to restrict the tourist traffic which had been disturbing the nesting sites.

But then, and although she would never know it, Tara's fortunes began to change. The fears and warnings of National Seashore Rangers, local and state Audubon tern wardens, and concerned environmentalists had at last been heard. All had claimed it was now too late to save the Least Tern. And if action was not taken immediately, the Cape would also soon see the last of the Arctic, Roseate, and eventually, the Common Tern.

Finally, authorities did what they should have done sooner and moved swiftly. For a five year period, all four and two wheeled vehicles were banished from the National Seashore beaches, and local ordinances were passed in Chatham, Orleans, Brewster, Dennis, Yarmouth and Barnstable. These ordinances strictly curtailed vehicular traffic on the town beaches.

But, Tara did not know this . . .

CHAPTER I

The two terns reached the western tip of Long Island ahead of schedule. Moving steadily eastward, they spent the next two days wandering back and forth across the island. The tiny estuaries and bays were generous, and they fed and played together with an intimate familiarity. This was understandable. It was their fourth season as breeding partners.

They were together constantly, calling back and forth while they chased each other across the easily recognized countryside. He was slightly larger than she and she let him lead the way. Mostly, they fed on small fish in the shallows, but sometimes they swooped low over the ripening coastal marshes and caught flying insects.

During the daylight hours they were aware of an awakening spring. Beneath their rapid wingbeats and undulating flight, Long Island was rousing from its winter hibernation. Patches of snow from an April blizzard still resisted the warming rays of a strengthening sun. The brush and scrub land were no longer naked. A slight tinge of green filled the shallow valley between the glacial moraines which wound easterly up the island from Queens. The northern one entered the sea at Orient Point, while the other disappeared beneath the water at Montauk. The southern part of the island was one large outwash plain consisting of truck farms and potato fields, which in summer would burst forth with a harvest of fresh vegetables. The southern shore was marshland country, and red-winged blackbirds were claiming territorial rights across the ripening salt hay and cord grass. From Coney Island to Southampton, the marshes were protected by long, narrow barrier beaches. The terns spent a few hours resting on Fire Island, which was a favored nesting place for some of their species.

They kept to themselves, talking back and forth with soft clucks. Sometimes, when they were resting, she would rub her beak against the side of his neck, and he would answer her with low, croaking sounds. Then she would bow her head submissively, almost in a begging posture. He would then fly out over the shallows and hover, waiting patiently. A sudden dive in and out of the water, and he would return, carrying the tiny fish to her. At other times they would reverse the procedure and she would feed him.

It was he who decided when they should continue onward. They ignored the other terns which were beginning to gather in colonies and continued moving eastward. Down below, silvery alewives were running up the narrow streams to inland ponds. Meanwhile, the gleaming yellow of the boisterous forsythia was flashing vividly across the countryside, and its proclamation that spring had arrived could not be denied.

The terns spent their last day on Long Island a mile west of Montauk Light. Both sensed that it was time to be moving on. The urge for coitus was growing stronger but they knew that this was not the time or the place. They were unaware of the forces affecting them, but their instincts told them what must be done.

Give or take a few days they should arrive at Nauset Spit on the fourth of May. Their biological clock dictated that coitus must occur about ten to fourteen days from now, while their celestial clock insisted that they must continue to follow the trajectory of the sun and keep pace with its northern journey. But to do this, they had to fix their position each evening by Polaris, the North Star, and Arcas, the Little Dipper.

The sun dipped behind Gardiner's Island, throwing a deep, purple-orange glow on globules of cumulus clouds. The two terns huddled together for warmth as the eastern sky darkened and as the evening air cooled rapidly. She moved closer against his body and they talked back and forth in muted tones, concerned about the possible appearance of great horned owls which preyed upon them. They pushed their bodies deeper into the cool sand. They were beyond the upper swash of the tide and had concealed themselves between thick clumps of new beach grass. As the darkness deepened, she stroked her beak along his folded wing. He murmured softly and she rested her head against his shoulder. She closed her eyes and dozed for a few moments.

He stayed awake, listening to the evening sounds for signs of danger. The air was almost calm but he could hear an occasional stirring in the surrounding beach grass. Fifty feet away, the water sighed wearily. The tide had been full an hour before and now was retreating weakly. A hundred yards to the west he could hear the subdued babble of a group of terns. The female shifted her position against his body slightly but continued dozing. She nuzzled her head against his shoulder. Montauk Light swept its beam spasmodically across the heavens. The male heard a familiar sound and looked skyward. Overhead, a four-engined jet climbed for altitude and headed for Europe.

He followed it until he could no longer see its lights or hear its sounds. Then he returned his stare to the stars. Almost forty-two degrees above the horizon, Polaris stared back at him. From it, the handle of the Little Dipper had reached the position he had been waiting for. The handle pointed due east for a short distance, then turned sharply upward before connecting with its tiny cup.

A few thin clouds skidded across the sky and the group of stars disappeared temporarily. When they reappeared, he roused her tenderly. She followed his gaze skyward. The configuration and location of the constellation filtered through their retinas and reached their simple brains. In some mysterious way Polaris and Arcas spanned light years of time and searched through their genes and they knew. Tomorrow they must arrive at Nauset Spit.

They crossed the eastern tip of Long Island the next morning at eight-thirty. Gardiner's Island gleamed like a piece of moist jade behind and below. On their right rear quarter Montauk Light rose from the cliff barely thirty-five feet from water's edge. The lighthouse was one of many landmarks which directed them towards the Cape.

Forty minutes later they passed over Block Island. Their heading was northeast and they were flying at an altitude of three thousand feet. She was flying off his right rear quarter at a distance of fifteen feet, and they called back and forth in clear, sharp, paired notes. They were not alone. They were a small part of a tidal wave of life whose northward migration was as certain as the new bits of existence it would produce.

As the minutes passed into hours they continued steadily on their course. To the north they could barely make out the Rhode Island coast sliding past them. It was covered by a heavy haze, which was surrendering grudgingly to a warm sun burning brightly in a clear eastern sky. Instinctively, they checked their position. Cuttyhunk Island lay dead ahead, the multicolored cliffs of Gay Head due east, and tiny Noman's Land to the southeast. They continued onward, flying over the southern coasts of the Elizabeth Islands whose inland woods were displaying the many shades of green produced by a ripening spring.

By early afternoon, the Elizabeth Islands and the Falmouth and Mashpee coastlines were behind them. As was their custom they dropped down wearily onto a mudflat in Centerville. It was time to feed and rest. Now they were among those of their own kind. Among those whose breeding home was Cape Cod. It was good to be back where they belonged, being surrounded by familiar sights and sounds. The flat was crowded with Common and Least Terns. Most had paired off and were feeding in the shallow waters. It was a loud and gregarious group, almost as if they were attending a family reunion. One minute they were flitting about nervously, the next moment alighting on the water, then rising quickly with a tiny fish. And all the time they were chattering back and forth with an agitated excitability. Chases would suddenly occur when one would steal food from the beak of another. Occasionally a male would spike his tail and point his beak skyward while he circled the female. But it was too early and he would be ignored.

The two terns kept to themselves while their courtship proceeded on schedule. They flew jauntily back and forth across the water, dipping down to it one moment, then rising rapidly as they passed the minnow back and forth. When the interplay was over they dropped back down onto the beach again. The sun was teasing forth new life in the nearby marsh and even their rudimentary sense of smell caught its rich, ripening aroma. A short distance away a second year herring gull stubbornly persisted in dropping a clam onto the soft sand. A black-backed gull soared effortlessly over head while a pair of spotted sandpipers flew past piping brightly with clear, shrill notes. They disappeared swiftly into the grass of a low dune where they would soon be nesting.

A Least Tern landed nearby and approached the terns. The male angered quickly and challenged the intruder, walking stiff-legged with his wings extended half way. He had the advantage because he was defending his mate. Sensing this, the intruder flew a short distance away, then called twice with his high-pitched voice, but offered no further challenge.

The terns fed for a few more moments, then decided it was time to go. It was an hour past mid-day and they wanted to be home by late afternoon. A short while later they were following the familiar coast eastward. Lewis Bay flowed past followed by other well-recognized landmarks. Then, as Great Island with its weatherbeaten cottages slipped slowly by beneath their right wings, the busy Bass River estuary appeared on their left. They called eagerly back and forth now as they pressed onward above the twisting sandy shoreline. The well-known sights and sounds of their breeding home was exerting a psychic effect on their pituitary glands, which in turn were pouring forth the hormones needed for urging onward their courtship ritual.

Over Wychmere Harbor she flew closer to him for a moment, called twice, then turned sharply toward Monomoy. He followed. Thirty minutes later they were cruising over the upper third of the island. A vague memory had drawn her here. Their nesting season the year before had been a failure. Their first try at Nauset Spit had failed when two campers had driven carelessly into their colony and remained there for three days. One had parked over their nest and they had been forced to abandon their eggs. In desperation they had tried again at Monomoy but their two chicks had been eaten alive by two black-crowned night herons.

The female had not forgotten. She circled their former nesting site while the male followed docilely. Hundreds of herring and black-backed gulls, which were nesting on the Atlantic side of the island, had taken over the beaches that the terns had been forced to abandon the year before. Long, blue-green breakers were rumbling onto the beach with an unceasing, dynamic symmetry. Their strength this day, however, was not intimidating, but instead they were collapsing weakly upon the steep foreshore before retreating into the foaming froth of the succeeding wave.

The two terns circled once more, riding a thin thermal from below. Then the female led her consort westerly across the greening dunes to the great expanse of lush marshland bordering Nantucket Sound. The four foot tide was ebbing and a broad mud flat was being exposed between the limits of the slack and flood tide. The female called once and the male followed her down, and for the next fifteen minutes, they fed on little gray minnows trapped in the shallow puddles.

Finally, the male grew impatient. When he rose from the flat and called to her, she reluctantly followed him and a short while later they were on a northern heading over the outer shore of North Beach. Pleasant Bay shimmered brightly in the late afternoon sun on their left, while to the seaward side, a few brave sailboats tacked doggedly against a local onshore breeze.

Once past Hog Island and Little Pleasant Bay, the two terns could see across Nauset Heights. Beyond the inlet, the Spit at the tip of Coast Guard Beach was teeming with recently arrived terns. The male had been flying a little above and ahead of the female and was first to recognize the familiar territory. As he did so, his excitement crested and he executed a quick wingover and stooped at her, calling loudly as he skidded past her tail. She responded with a harsh cry of approval and followed him, imitating his every move. First he swooped down over the beach, then did a twisting, climbing turn for altitude. She was with him all the way and when he finished whirling through a double barrel roll, she duplicated it with a deft precision. A moment later they began diving and stooping at each other, all the time maintaining a northerly course toward their final destination. He did a nervous, climbing figure eight, calling excitedly with a voice more urgent and gutteral. Then he descended low over Nauset inlet and hovered, standing expertly against the easterly breeze, his primaries feathering the air with rapid strokes. A sudden dip into the water and he was in the air again. They were surrounded by other Least Terns and when a male tried to take the silverbait from him he angered quickly. The female darted up from below and pecked the intruder harshly. He loosened his grip and flew away, the female chasing him for a short distance. When she returned, she rose up on the port side of the male and he passed the silverbait to her. She slid away a few feet, then closed the distance between them and offered it back to him. He refused and she ate it in one gulp, then dropped down among the others. He followed.

Once on the ground, they searched busily, flying haphazardly for short distances in all directions until their instincts brought them to the area they had occupied the year before. It was just beyond the upper limit of the last flood tide, a stony portion of the beach bounded on the south by a large, barkless log. A third year male, unsure of himself, had instinctively occupied the region, not knowing why. The male chased him away. The twelve yards of beach was theirs. He gave the female a gentle peck. She bowed her head submissively. Their courtship began in earnest.

They were home.

CHAPTER II

The two terns were Tara's parents. They spent the next ten days in courtship while the spit clamored with over fifty pairs of Least Terns and hundreds of Common Terns, all engaged in the same ritual. Also, scattered throughout the ternery were a few pairs of Roseate Terns and one pair of Arctic Terns.

Tara's life began on May fifteenth, nineteen hundred and seventy-three when her parents copulated in the late afternoon shadows of sixteen-foot high dunes, which guarded a foreshore swept clean by a recent spring tide. Three tiny ova, each smaller than a grain of sand and surrounded by a covering of rich, orange yolk, had erupted through the surface of the female's ovary and had entered her oviduct. Following copulation, millions of wiggling, squirming spermatozoa had traveled up this oviduct searching for their destiny. Three had been successful. The beginning of Tara was the result of the first of these three unions.

As the fertilized eggs descended along the oviduct, they were coated with a thick covering of albumin. Then they passed through glands which encased each of them with two sinewy membranes that were necessary to keep the albumin separated from the shell. Following this, and for the next twenty hours, the formless eggs passed through the shell gland where liquid shell with its characteristic color pigments enclosed them. Finally, thirty hours after copulation, Tara's mother began laying the eggs, one each day. The shells hardened as the eggs passed through her cloaca to the outside and into a shallow depression which she had hollowed with her breast during the final stages of courtship.

Actually, Tara and her two brothers had begun developing before they left the warmth and security of their mother's body. These early beginnings had been halted temporarily, however, while the two adults spent the first twenty-four hours lining the tiny depression with bits of broken shell and pieces of seaweed. These actions were the result of a brief instinctive urge to camouflage the eggs. The three eggs were small, barely over an inch long, but large in proportion to the female's body. Two of them were pale green and spotted with varying shades of brown, while Tara's shell was the color of light sand splashed with pale lavendar markings.

Although Tara would never know it, a calamity struck the clutch early. Three days into the brooding period, an early morning jogger was running along the hardpacked foreshore while his large Doberman plowed aimlessly through the colony. The hysterical terns went into a rage and tried desperately to drive the intruder away. Screaming harshly, they dive-bombed him repeatedly, some even defecating on him. But on he came. Others tried in vain to distract him by repeatedly flying off and on their nests. Tara's father even succeeded in pecking him painfully behind the ear, but still he continued onward, scattering eggs and terns in all directions. The jogger, of course, was unaware of the significance of all this and continued innocently on his way. What would have been Tara's two brothers were destroyed by the left rear paw of the dog. The animal, however, was only one reason for a decrease in tern productivity by the colony that year. But Tara was one of the fortunate. She was one of those who survived.

For the next twelve days she grew rapidly while all of the albumin and most of the yolk was transformed into her being. Even the shell grew thinner because most of its calcium and lime were used to form her miniscule skeleton.

It was on the seventeenth day of incubation that she inhaled her first breath. Her father was brooding the egg for a few moments while her mother was splashing in the gentle surf. Upon returning, she rotated the egg carefully, and for the first time Tara became aware of her frail prison and opened her eyes. Light filtered through the fragile shell and membranes. She opened her beak and tried to peep, but couldn't. She tried once more without success. The egg turned again and she rolled over onto her back. Her oxygen supply from the yolk was diminishing rapidly. Instinctively she pushed her egg tooth against the transparent sheath. It stretched, but refused to yield. She braced her feet against the shell and pushed again. The sheath tore a little. She needed oxygen desperately. She pushed again. The gap widened. She pushed harder. This time she sawed through both sheaths and suddenly oxygen rushed into her lungs from the inner air sac. She inhaled deeply, then peeped loudly a few times. Her parents answered with rapid "kikiki" sounds. She answered them once, then fell asleep to regain her strength. Tomorrow there was much to be done.

When she awoke twelve hours later, the inside of the egg was dark. When she began peeping again, her mother hopped off the egg excitedly and called the male. He had finished feeding her a few moments earlier and now he was feeding himself. He rushed back to her, gulping down a minnow as he landed by her side. She nudged the egg again with the top of her bill. Tara peeped once more. The male jumped up and down flapping his wings joyously. Then the female settled onto the egg and Tara began the second in-

Brooding the egg

stinctive act of her young life.

The egg tooth reached upward from the top of her bill. The challenging shell lay above and the instinct surged through her body. She stretched her short neck and touched the shell hesitantly. The slight scraping action excited her and she rubbed more vigorously. She felt the beginning of the groove. This encouraged her and she gained confidence as these early moments passed. Then she gained strength and worked with increasing power. But even so, she was forced to stop from time to time and rest.

It took her three and one half hours to make the first star-shaped crack. Finally, she pipped the egg and then she slept for an hour. Her mother had felt the vibrating action against her brooding spot while Tara had been busy, but now the egg lay quiet. She moved away from the egg and watched it solemnly. Her father was there also. From this point onward, neither of them would touch it.

It was late afternoon when Tara began working again. She worked on and off for the next twenty-four hours, and by mid-afternoon of the following day, she had completed five more of these star-shaped cracks. They more than half-circled the egg and now she was finished. During these last twenty-four hours, the yolk sac which had been attached to her underside was gradually absorbed by her stomach, and for an hour she lay quietly while her skin closed over the opening. She rested for fifteen more minutes. She was damp and distressed, and for the first time in seventeen days she was not receiving any nourishment. The first signs of hunger were appearing. She inserted her beak into the crack and pushed. It parted slightly. She pushed again, closing her eyes against the glare of the sun as the crack widened. Her parents watched in silence and waited patiently.

A yearling herring gull mottled with brown approached the western perimeter of the colony. The male jumped into the air with some other males, chased it away, then they called harshly to each other, satisfied with their efforts. When he returned to the shallow, pebble-lined nest in the sand, Tara was breaking through the shell.

She collapsed momentarily, lying half in and half out of it. When she opened her eyes and saw her parents for the first time, she gave a weak peep signalling recognition. But she knew instinctively that they would not help her until she was free of the shell. This was the way it was. This was the way it had to be. She pushed against the ground with her wet, stubby wings and pulled away from the shell. Her moist down lay stuck to her fragile body as she rested in the warm, soft sand. She closed her eyes for a few moments. Her mother clucked reassuringly to her and covered her with her wing. She lay quietly while her down dried to a fluffy softness, and listened to the muted, pleased talk of her parents. Once she peeked out from beneath the safety of her mother's feathers and watched her father when he picked up pieces of shell and disposed of them behind a windrow of eel grass. His instinct told him to remove the pieces away from the nest because their white lining could be seen by the sharp eyes of flying predators.

An hour later she was able to stand weakly on short, stubby legs. She was hungry now and she began letting her parents know it by complaining with feeble cheeps which grew stronger with each passing moment. She was fortunate. The deaths of her two brothers meant she would not have to compete for food. Her parents would not have to deal with the inevitable distractions of caring for more than one chick and therefore she would receive their complete attention.

Her mother spoke to her father in a subdued tone and a moment later he was flying toward the inlet. He was gone for twenty minutes and when he returned he had a tiny minnow in his beak. He landed lightly at the edge of the nest and passed it to her mother. As soon as Tara saw it she opened her beak wide. Her peeping tone was demanding now. Her mother shoved the fish headfirst into her mouth and Tara swallowed greedily. She called for more. Five times her father repeated the procedure. Finally, as the evening sun settled slowly behind the high dunes marking the spine of the Spit, her father brought a three inch sand eel to her mother. Three more times he fed her, and when she refused the fourth, he fed himself.

Later that evening, after a moonless darkness had crept across the crooked land, Tara received an impression upon her genes which would guide her until she died. Instinctively, she raised her tiny head toward the heavens and followed the stare of her parents. From this time onward she would be aware of one group of stars only. The rest would have no meaning to her, but Polaris and the Little Bear would capture her essence, become part of her celestial clock, and serve as her navigator.

At birth Tara weighed a bare third of an ounce and was little more than an inch long. Once her down was dry she appeared no larger that a small marshmallow: a furry little piece of life whose upper surface was the same color as the marbled sand of her nest and with a few irregular brownish-black spots across the top of her head, back and rump. Her underparts were white to buff but with a deeper buffy hue on her throat. Her bill was a pale yellow-tan, as were her feet and legs.

Nature had endowed her with a voracious appetite necessary to maintain her rapid energy processes. Her heartbeat was much faster than that of larger vertebrates and her body temperature much higher. Because of this she called for food constantly. It was so dictated by the life that she was born into that she should fly in three to four weeks' time. This was necessary for a number of

Tara

reasons. One was that she was more vulnerable on the ground than she was in the air. Another was that she must be ready to migrate in two months' time.

Unlike the Common or Roseate Tern chicks, she was off and running the next day, all the time calling constantly for food. She learned quickly to defecate away from the nest, and her weary parents fed and brooded her where they found her. Like all tern chicks, she led a charmed life. She had to, to survive. And she was fortunate not to have to pay with her life for the mistakes that she made. She could hardly be seen as she ran to and fro across the warm, dry sand, peeping loudly, and this invisibility was a means of protection which nature had given her.

Only once did she wander into the territory of another Least Tern pair, but her mother's warning cry called her out of danger before the nesting female could react to her presence. She could have been pecked harshly, and if the attacker's beak had found her fragile skull, she would have died instantly.

In the middle of the third day of her life she learned another lesson of survival. She had wandered away from the nest momentarily while she had digested a sand eel. It had been a bit too large for her to swallow completely, so she sat quietly, looking quite ridiculous with its tail sticking out of her mouth while her stomach digested the head. Finally, she was able to gulp down the rest and as she did so, six herring gulls sailed in effortlessly on silent wings from the northwest and across the upper ridge of the dunes. Her mother saw them first and screamed the warning cry. Terror raced through Tara's miniscule brain, but an instinct which was centuries old and which needed no reasoning power told her what to do. Instantly, she flattened out on the sand and closed her eyes. Her heart was racing even faster than usual. She pressed her body into the sand and listened to the slaughter taking place, unable to shut it out from her hearing.

She would never forget those terrifying sounds. All about her was the harsh screaming of the entire colony as they reacted to the sudden tragedy. They attacked the gulls on all sides in angry, high-pitched squawks. They lashed out desperately at the silver-winged predators which were their larger cousins and whose instinct told them there were mouthfuls of furry bits of protein now available on the beach. All of the chicks, Least, Common and Roseate, flattened out on the ground while their parents joined forces to meet the common threat. After a few moments of listening to the ghastly sounds of frantic fighting, the gulls were routed and Tara heard the agitated calls of the adult terns as they searched for their offspring. Fifteen had disappeared in the melee, eaten alive by the marauding gulls. Death was instantaneous for those unlucky chicks whose delicate skulls were crushed swiftly by the strong beaks of their persistent pursuers.

Those terns which lost their chicks would leave the colony in a few days and try elsewhere, while those with survivors would become more cautious and vigilant in their mission to bring their remaining chicks to the fledgling stage. But now the ternery was a frantic mass of screaming, disorganized confusion. Adults were everywhere, searching for their young, calling back and forth in anxious, high-pitched voices, scolding one another for inadvertently entering their territory, fluttering haphazardly across the dunes, recognizing chicks they thought were theirs, then realizing their error.

Tara heard all of this but didn't move, instead remaining frozen to the ground. Twice a tern landed nearby and looked her over. Each one called to her but their voices were not the ones she responded to. She remained still and silent. She had strayed twenty yards from the nest and was near the lower line of beach grass anchoring the dunes. Then she heard a familiar voice some distance away, and quivered when she recognized it as that of her mother. It was coming closer and at the same time she heard the authoritative voice of her father. When they landed close by and spoke to her with reassuring and comforting mewing-like sounds, she opened her eyes and raised her head, but still remained motionless. They spoke to her soothingly, telling her that the threat was over. She stood up, still trembling, and they led her back to the nest, one on each side of her. She forgot about food for the remainder of the day and her mother brooded her beneath her wing while her father roosted nearby on the gray-weathered log.

It was an unfortunate law of nature that those who died increased the chances of survival of those who didn't. And so it was with Tara and the other chicks. For the next three weeks, the adults exhausted themselves as they struggled tirelessly to feed their complaining, demanding young. Tara was no different. In fact, she was even more belligerent than the others as her loud peeps beat endlessly against her parents' ears. They fed her continuously. When she wasn't eating, she was constantly running about, preferring to get her exercise in the hard-packed sand of the tire tracks left by campers and dunebuggies. At other times she was at the edge of the dunes visiting with those Common and Roseate chicks who were more cautious than she in their travels, preferring to remain closer to their nests.

All the while, her parents kept a close watch on her. Three times more she flattened out in the sand when she heard the warning cries of her parents: once when a marsh hawk flew over the inlet; another time when a black-backed gull soared low along the water line; and lastly for no apparent reason when the entire colony took to one of their numerous "dread" flights out over the water.

In the meantime she grew rapidly. By the end of her first week she had doubled her weight to two thirds of an ounce and was two inches long. A week later she had doubled her weight again. Her primary concern, of course, was for food. That, and the instinct to fly. It was her habit to beat her stubby, down-covered wings up and down rapidly whenever she took time out from running, and this was usually when she was calling for food.

Even so, it was also a time for learning. Her celestial clock had an inbred mechanism which enabled her to locate Polaris and the Little Bear each evening at eight o'clock. She had to know when it was eight o'clock in order for her to follow Little Bear's counterclockwise rotation around Polaris. Each night at this hour the constellation was approximately one degree further counter-clockwise than it was the previous evening. It was her parents who provided the necessary teaching for Tara to use this profound instinct whose mystique would forever be unintelligible to man. Each night at this hour she listened attentively to the throaty instructions of her parents. Tara was truly fortunate, for they were more intelligent than the average Least Tern and they had passed this on to her.

Her world was small these first few weeks and although she was continually preoccupied with her nutritional needs, she still found time to explore the beach. How many centuries had its spinning sands been on the march? The winds and waves have taken their toll upon the more fragile substances and now Tara's domain glittered with bits of quartz, feldspar, magnetite and garnets. Interspersed with all of this were crushed bits of shell from scallops, snails, oysters and clams. Curiously, she poked her beak into broken egg cases of skates, and sand hopper holes along the upper beach, then examined the empty shells of horseshoe crabs, which had been carried onto the beach by the tide.

With the changing season, the character of the wild, winter Atlantic was softening. Then, it had cut and carved the pliant shore with a fierce intensity, creating a sharply climbing, narrow beach which had stiffened stubbornly against the vicious onslaught. But now the temper of the great ocean was changing. It was becoming more subdued and it was treating its margins more gently. The result was a broad, sloping sandspit more amenable to its spring and summer tasks.

Tara was more at ease along the upper tide line which she explored with the other Least Tern chicks and those Common and Roseate chicks who dared to venture from the comforting covering of the grass-covered dunes. With them, she discovered willowy windrows of eel grass which had been torn from beneath the sea by the rugged breakers. Tough, gristly Irish Moss and glossy, bright green sea lettuce along with plentiful brownish kelp also aroused her curiosity. And always she was startled when she inadvertently flushed the sandhoppers and greenhead flies from the decaying seaweed.

In the meantime, her parents watched her carefully, her mother sheltering her from the burning sun when necessary while her father labored constantly to maintain the supply of shrimp and fish. By the end of her third week, dramatic changes had taken place. She had increased her weight by almost seven times, weighing two and one-half ounces and measuring almost four inches in length. But something else had happened.

By the end of the second week, she had begun losing her down, and at this time her first flight feathers appeared when they began pushing through her flesh. This process continued rapidly during the third week when her young body underwent an intensive growth and development. As the fourth week began, she was a little less than two thirds the size of her parents, quite plump and vigorous, and physically able to fly, although she had not yet learned how. She was no longer a downy young, but even so, her pre-fledgling appearance bore no resemblance to the new-born chick of three weeks before.

The region around her eyes, ears and nape was a dark gray, almost black, while the top of her head and scapulars were a deep tan, which hid the light gray of her upper plumage. The remainder of her back and rump had become a dark, mottled brown, sprinkled liberally with dark, irregular markings. The sides of her neck and upper breast had retained the buff color of the nestling, but the remainder of her underparts had changed to that of a more off-white. Her tail was quite short and gray-colored, with its outer margins somewhat lighter. Her feet and legs were a drab yellow as was her bill, which was accentuated with a dark tip. Her primary flight feathers were gray, becoming progressively lighter as they approached her secondaries, which were almost white.

Meanwhile, the colony had become a disorderly mass of confusion. The near fledglings were experiencing the flocking instinct and more often than not they played and exercised in groups of five to ten in number. During this period of their growth, they were drawn to the water line, and it was here that Tara cavorted with the others, getting her feet wet, splashing her growing wings in the water, outrunning most incoming waves, but sometimes not being quite fast enough and being tumbled over and over when it swept her short legs out from under her. But each time she would get up quickly and shake herself, exulting in this carefree time of her life.

The adults were in constant motion, complaining with a medley of cackling and whistling sounds. There was a continual flying about as they moved in and out of their territory with seemingly no rhyme or reason. And as always, the chicks called incessantly for food, becoming more strident as their fast-growing bodies needed a larger and larger food supply with each passing day. The adults were exhausting themselves as they struggled with this ordeal. Fortunately for all concerned, there was an abundance of food this year: sand eels, minnows and killifish were available in the inlet, while shrimp were plentiful along the shimmering, twisting tidal creeks of Nauset marsh.

But even so, there was constant turmoil as the lazier terns tried stealing from the others, some even going so far as to wait until a chick had been fed and then stealing the fish from its bill. Not so with Tara. She lashed out savagely at the young adult in its fourth summer and sent it screaming in frustration across the frothy tops of the incoming breakers.

And all the time Tara's small brain was receiving endless impressions while her world continued to expand. How many times did her mother or father spot a minnow while she watched them carefully? As they flew above the surface with their bright yellow bills pointing vertically downward, they instinctively searched the water for the glistening flashes of the darting, tiny fish. Then, upon seeing their prey, they would descend in quick, swirling spirals until they were just above the surface. Here they would hover, their long, graceful wings beating just fast enough to maintain a stationary position. Suddenly, they would dive into the water, at times pulling their wings in close to their bodies like gannets, and going completely under. Upon their breaking through the surface, the minnow would be clasped firmly in their bill, if they had been lucky, and Tara would let fly with her rasping, demanding calls. 'Ki-ki-ki,'' she would screech with her high-pitched voice until one or the other pushed it into her gaping mouth.

It was during this eventful fourth week of her life that summer appeared. The sun hovered briefly over the Tropic of Cancer and warmed the sandy beaches, then, almost reluctantly, began its at first imperceptible, but then steady, six months return journey to the Tropic of Capricorn in the Southern Hemisphere. In the meantime, Tara's domain displayed its appreciation for the increasing warmth. Hardy sandwort sprinkled its tiny white flowers across the barren beach in dainty contrast to its coarse, fleshy leaves, while a fresh growth of sea rocket colonized the beach in timeless triumph, and burst forth with its pale purple flowers. Dusty miller was sprouting soon-to-be-tall stalks above its furry gray-green leaves and if one looked closely, the first hint of yellow of its July flowers was reminiscent of pitch pine pollen floating on the upland ponds in mid-spring.

But there were other signs. Traffic was increasing steadily along the Cape roads. Marinas had reopened. Fishing boats and catamarans were appearing in the estuaries, inlets and bays, while beach vehicles were multiplying all along the awakening shore. The tourists were coming, descending upon the fragile land in direct proportion to its increasing warmth. To accommodate them, restaurants, motels, shops, nightclubs and all sorts of entertainment were either reopening or expanding for the coming season.

With each passing year, new construction was keeping pace with the demands of an increasing winter and summer population. And as it did so, more marshes were being drained to be replaced by beachfront resort property and marinas. All of this led to the construciton of new landfill dumps for refuse and garbage, which further intensified the exploding herring gull community. The result was an inexorable and steady displacement of the terns from their traditional island colonies. They in turn were forced to the less desirable barrier beaches where they were preyed upon by skunks, foxes, weasels and . . . man.

Tara would never understand the whys and wherefores. She would, however, like the others, experience the frustrations of continual breeding failures, and because of this, fewer Least Terns would return to the Cape each year, until finally, there would be only one.

But right now, in the fourth week of her life, she was obsessed with one driving force, and that was to fly. Ten days before, she had experienced the unfamiliar sensation for the first time. She had been exceptionally active, even for a Least Tern chick, constantly running about, skittering between clumps of beach grass, sometimes hiding in its shade to get away from the direct rays of the sun. And she was forever flapping her stubby wings as she scampered about. Her wing muscles strengthened steadily as the days sped by and she was exhilarated when she felt her body lighten while spreading her wings into the summer wind.

Then one day, while she was waiting for food, she was standing at the water line and looking into a brisk, onshore breeze. She had gauged the temper of the waves perfectly, and was just beyond their swash. It was early morning and she was alone on the desolate beach, the other chicks still sleeping securely near their parents. She was waiting impatiently for her own who were beyond the slight curve of the beach at the inlet, and she was bouncing up and down, peeping loudly in anticipation of the start of breakfast.

Suddenly her mother came into sight, skimming low across the waves, her speed deceptively fast in contrast to her slow-beating wings. When Tara saw her with the tiny shrimp in her bill, she became even more excited and flapped her wings spiritedly. Just as she was doing this, the wind freshened momentarily, streamed across the slight concave curvature of her wings, and for a few brief moments she floated upward. For a moment she experienced fear at this new dimension, but then she heard the encouraging calls of her mother. She fluttered up and down like a yo-yo for a few moments, but when the wind died, she dropped quickly into the water for an unexpected and unwanted bath.

For the next two days, both parents spent most of the time persuading her to fly. Their main tactic was to tease her with food. No longer was it given without hesitation. Instead, they flew about her in tight circles, calling to her with prompting "kik-kik-kik" sounds, while they held fish or shrimp in their bills. Each time they did this, Tara responded with more confidence, at first rising higher each time for longer periods, but gradually flying for short distances toward the prize which they held. And all the time her calls and those of the other pre-fledglings echoed across the blooming dunes and heralded the anticipation of their first flight.

It came first for Tara. Her father had just given her a fat minnow and had then started again for the inlet. She swallowed the food in one gulp and began following him for what she thought would be the usual short flight. But as she lifted into the air, a steady flow of wind sprang up from the south and strengthened quickly. In an instant she was buoyed upward effortlessly; and then instead of flapping her wings up and down, she began bringing them forward in sweeping, awkward, downward strokes. Instinctively now, she twisted her outer primaries like miniature propellors and throughout the downward stroke, they bit firmly into the flowing air. Then on the upstroke, she pitched them in such a way as to offer the least air resistance until they almost touched high above her body before sweeping down and forward again. Her inner wings from her wrists to her scapulars did not move through as great an arc as did her primaries but instead provided the necessary lift for her to remain afloat in this "river of air." It was all really very simple. As she was thrust forward by her propellor-like primaries, the air flowed faster across the upper convex surface of her wing than it did across the flatter lower surface. The decrease in air pressure produced by the faster air flow across the upper surface in combination with the increased air pressure on the lower surface gave her wing the lift needed to buoy her upward.

So up she went for the first time, calling nervously to her mother who was by her side screaming encouragement. Tara veered clumsily toward the waves, her instinct telling her that if she was going to fall she should fall into the water. Fortunately, she had all the room she needed to maneuver as she flew toward the inlet. She was all over the sky, up and down, when the wind slackened momentarily, and swerving drunkenly from side to side as she attempted spunkily to bring some coordination to this new experience. Around the curve of the beach she came, calling anxiously and trying to figure out how she would land. She had a fleeting glimpse of her father down below. He was standing near the edge of the marsh and he held a fat, squirming shrimp in his bright yellow, black-tipped bill. He called to her with a musical "pee-dee, pee-dee."

Her first landing was certainly not what one would call expert, but it got her down. She simply stopped flapping her wings and plopped into the water. Then she turned and faced her parents and uttered a hearty call which was a mixture of hunger, elation and satisfaction. The male gave his new fledgling the shrimp while the female shouted her approval.

CHAPTER III

July with its increasing warmth and shortening days greeted the new fledgling. The foredunes of Nauset Spit had been well worn by beach traffic the year before, but beach grass was now battling successfully to repair the damage. Its long underground stems were drawing increasing strength from its deep, moisture-seeking roots, and the newborn shoots of April which had sprung from nodules beneath the surface had now matured into tough, coarse blades which bent before the wind and traced perfect half circles in the sand. The were the prime defender against beach erosion and they struggled tirelessly to stabilize the dune in preparation for the less rugged pioneers.

One of these was beach pea, whose ground-hugging vines zigzagged boldly between clumps of beach grass and flung upward foot-high shoots which erupted jauntily all through summer with clusters of pink and lavender flowers. Alongside the beach pea and near the crest of the dunes, seaside goldenrod was flourishing on thick, nodular stems, but was not yet ready to flower.

Tara was not interested in this floral display and she ignored also the spirited blooming of beach heather and dusty miller which displayed their bright yellow flowers like drops of liquid gold across the valleys between the dunes. And she was also too busy learning how to fly to appreciate the blossoming of the fragrant pink and white flowers of salt spray rose which anchored the secondary dunes along with patches of low-growing bearberry and two-foot tall scrub oak and pitch pine trees.

By the second week in July, she was in the air from dawn to dusk except when she was feeding. Her parents were faithfully by her side at all times. Most of the young birds were flying by this time, but for the next two weeks their parents continued with the arduous task of helping them perfect their flying skills. In addition, the fledglings were still dependent upon their parents for food, and would remain so until they completed their long journey to South America in the fall.

Tara improved her flying expertise by watching and imitating the older terns. She followed them endlessly and when they wanted to catch a few moments' rest, she refused to let them do so, calling at them impatiently, sometimes even going so far as to peck at them angrily until they reluctantly returned to the air. As the days passed, she learned how to take off into the wind and how to land smoothly by stroking her wings in the reverse direction in order to provide the necessary braking action. She was taught how to use her forked tail both as a rudder for banking turns and as a stabilizer for the maintenance of level flight when the wind was unpredictably gusty. She discovered how to use her wings in slow, steady, deep strokes for distant flights, and how to chop through the air with quick, erratic thrusts when developing her adroit, nimble maneuverability.

It did not take her long to learn that a following wind gave her more speed, but less lift, while a head wind exerted greater lifting power at the cost of a decrease in speed. In the meantime, her parents taught her how to search for and find the rising thermals, and she learned quickly how to slip their grasp and descend effortlessly in graceful spiraling circles. More often than not, because she was so daring, she would ride them to their maximum altitude before sliding reluctantly away to began her earthward call.

It was at these higher altitudes that she barrel-rolled through the wispy clouds and practiced fast-climbing figure eight turns. She was elated by this challenging new domain, and for as long as she lived would claim it as hers alone except for those Herculean four months in late spring and summer when her genes would summon her back to the sandy, unpredictable beaches.

She was taught how to bring one wing closer to her body than the other, and to sideslip deftly downward when she needed a rapid, curving descent, and she sought gleefully the new-found thrill of stooping, or diving rapidly earthward when she pulled both wings close against her body. And how she enjoyed standing effortlessly with the wind in her face hundreds of feet above the ground. The lifting effect of the breeze flowing across her outstretched wings while she feathered the air clumsily with her extended primaries filled her with a timeless feeling of freedom and independence which would be the primary motivating factors in her twelve years of earthly life. But as the days of July grew shorter, she was neither free nor independent.

It was at this time when a subtle restlessness came over those adults who had successfully raised their chicks to the fledgling stage. Now, they and the juveniles were foraging across the countryside. The beginning of the adults' postnuptial molt indicated the regression of their gonads, while younger birds were also showing signs of change. Some of them, like Tara, were almost as large as

Tara

their parents and in August they wore their first winter plumage.

Tara could be told from her parents only by the expert. The front and top of her head was now a grayish white, although somewhat whiter toward her bill, which was a dusky gray. Her nape was a confused mixture of black, gray and brown, while her mantle and underparts were similar to those of her parents except for a grayish-black band at the bend of each wing. Finally, her legs and feet had become a dull, almost dirty yellow.

On the first day of August at eight in the evening, Arcas, the Little Bear, was pointing straight up in the northern sky and was about to begin its three month sweep from north to west. Its signal to Tara and her parents was not as mighty as it had been in midwinter, but in combination with the decreasing amount of daylight, it told them it was time to begin fattening up for the southward migration.

Throughout her fledgling period, Tara's parents had been feeding her while she was learning to fly. But now, as their foraging took them farther away from the colony, they encouraged her to fish and hunt for her own food. She discovered that this was not easy. First she had to locate the small fry swimming just below the surface, which was difficult enough; but to hover and dive into the water for a successful catch was close to impossible. But she kept at it doggedly, and gradually she learned how. In the meantime, her parents made sure she was well-fed and her ever increasing weight testified to this.

Then one day in late August, the flock of terns left the colony and did not return. It was time to go. Seaside goldenrod had flowered along the dunes, the first harbinger of a changing season, while the tiny, snow-white flowers of sea-beach sandwort had gone by and were hanging lifeless from their thick, green stems. In the marsh, the hearty green of summer was disappearing and the first touch of its late summer hues of gold and russet was greeting the arrival of greater yellowlegs which were passing through from their nesting grounds on the northern tundra to their winter homes along the Gulf coast. The tall, willowy marsh grasses appeared to be inviting them earthward to feed on the abundant fish and insect life in their teeming, twisting tidal creeks. Bordering the marshes like a delicate lavender lace trimming on a curtain were dainty, fragrant flowers of marsh rosemary. Each spray capped a solitary, leafless, branching stem whose thick, rounded leaves grew out from the root and lay on the ground in a rosette.

Tara and her parents drifted lazily southward with the others, foraging for food by day and roosting by night on the flats and sandbars. Two weeks later they had reached Cuttyhunk. The sense of urgency that had existed in their spring migration was not present at this time of year. In the meantime, Tara continued to grow and learn. She was now almost as large as her parents and was feeding herself most of the time.

A week later they reached the western tip of Fire Island and here they dawdled for a few days. Each evening at eight they calculated the position of Arcas, and each dawn they showed Tara how to measure the distance the sun had traveled along the eastern horizon. It was their nature to keep pace with it as their migration continued.

Three days later they dropped down at the edge of a marsh near Cape May. The two mile boardwalk of the resort area showed the wear and tear of a busy summer while some of the rental cottages were shuttered for the winter. Here, a hundred years ago, the marshes and tidal flats had swarmed with thousands of terns, but since then, most of the marshes had been drained for land development while the natural beaches had been transformed for the pleasures of vacationers.

Tara looked up from her feeding when she heard a different tone in her father's chattering. She and her mother followed his gaze skyward. Four thousand feet above, a peregrine falcon was winging his way south. His nesting season northwest of Hudson Bay had ended in failure. His mate had been old and had ingested too much DDT for too many years and her thin-shelled eggs had cracked right after laying. Then, shortly after they had begun their migration, the old female had died in the air over James Bay.

Tara and the others need not fear the falcon this day. An hour before, he had fed on a blue jay near Ocean City, and now he wanted to make another hundred miles on his migration to Key West before resting for the night.

By the end of their third week of migration, and as the sun passed over the equator, Tara and her parents were at the Pea Island National Wildlife Refuge, a section of the Outer Banks of Cape Hatteras. The rich, lush marshes bordering Pamlico Sound had been waiting patiently for the Canada geese, snow geese and whistling swans who were now arriving for the winter. Tara and the others lingered for a few days, feeding leisurely on the shores of Pamlico Sound during the day and roosting in the dunes at night.

Each dawn they were up before the sun watching the dark eastern sky turn pasty gray, followed by a sweeping whiteness which surrendered meekly to fuzzy shafts of orange spreading outward above the horizon like an oriental fan. Then the huge fiery globe would heave itself out of a blue-green ocean and color the frothy whiteness of the seven foot breakers with its ocher-colored rays.

A day later they were at Cape Hatteras when the weather changed. The ocean waters became dirty gray colored while the clear azure sky, which had been serving up globules of eastward-drifting, snow-white cumulus clouds, began to mirror the temper of the Atlantic. Beneath a deepening heavy overcast, low-flying, rain-leadened clouds began scudding in from the southeast.

The flock of terns became restless as did the other southward migrating shorebirds. Pairs of plump willets glanced nervously skyward, while ruddy turnstones paused in their unique method of feeding, and called to each other with paired, throaty whistles. Chubby, black-bellied plovers in their autumn plumage of mottled pale-gray above and white underparts were becoming uneasy as they finished feeding in the restless marsh, and gathered in large flocks on the barrier beach bordering Pamlico Sound. Dark brown, short-billed dowitchers paused apprehensively from time to time in their up and down probing along the swash, while knots who were of the same size and color but with a shorter bill, kept company with the black-bellied plovers.

As late afternoon approached, the wind freshened and became more easterly, and the huge ocean swells so aptly associated with Cape Hatteras took on a more threatening tone as they broke across the outlying sandbars and began thundering across the upper beach. Gradually at first, but then more rapidly, the birds disappeared into heavy thickets of beach grass onto the higher ground of marsh country.

Tara felt the decreasing pressure in her ears, unable to understand its significance, or the nervous, high-pitched chattering of the older terns. Then when her parents alighted nearby and called sharply to her, she followed them without hesitation. She was somewhat apprehensive now and a little fearful. With her father leading the way and her mother bringing up the rear, the three of them skimmed through the low valleys between the dunes, flying southerly as they fought the gusting wind on their left quarter. Tara's eyes were stinging from sand and salt spray, which the wind was whipping viciously from the crest of the higher dunes and huge, lumbering waves. She had never flown in such unpredictable air currents before, but her youth and strength coupled with a stubborn courage made up for her inexperience. Ten minutes later they rose above the crest of a forty foot dune. She was startled by the power of the wind and was forced to use all of her strength to ward off a sudden downdraft which almost tumbled her into the sand. But the sight of an unexpected stand of trees directly ahead toughened her resolve, and a few moments later they were beneath a thicket at the edge of a shallow fresh water pond.

Buxton Woods was their savior. The three thousand acre forest at the southern end of Hatteras Island is an odd mixture of robust oak, holly and dogwood trees in combination with dense, vine-infested thickets of shrubbery amidst outcroppings of marsh.

For the next twelve hours until the hurricane passed, life stood still on the Outer Banks. Cattails bordering the upper edges of marshes, cordgrass, and tall, willowy stalks of sea oats surrendered weakly to the tormenting wind and lay broken on the ground.

Tara lay close to her parents and listened. The wind came roaring through the trees, whistling and whining while small branches broke away and blew inland. Larger branches snapped like twigs and rattled through the lower limbs while an occasional dead or dying tree gave up the struggle and fell to the ground, its shallow roots agonizing like old, scraggy fingers. Meanwhile, blowing sand blasted the tormented leaves, was trapped by them, and then filtered down with the salty rain to the littered floor below.

On rare occasions when the wind velocity dropped momentarily, Tara could hear the breakers. Pushed by an assaulting wall of wind, the fourteen-foot storm waves began breaking across the outer sandbars and chewed up the shallow waters. Where the beach was broad and flat, the dirty, gray-brown breakers spilled across the sand and inundated sea rocket and seaside spruce. In those areas where the beach narrowed, the battering rams of water boomed against and gnawed away at the dune cliffs, exposing roots of beach grass anchoring broken blades which now lay flat. And, as had been happening for hundreds of years, the wind and water shaped and transformed the barrier beaches. New inlets to Pamlico Sound were created while others were closed off. Sandbars moved. Dunes marched farther into Buxton Woods. Other dunes became valleys, while valleys became dunes. At the Cape itself, where the two-hundred-foot light towers bravely into the gale as if it were a sentinel guarding the eastward-pointing two mile spit of sand, the monumental storm waves broke and frothed like magnified whitecaps. As they did, the sea flaunted once again its awesome power and invincibility.

The storm passed the following day and the terns continued on their way. The remainder of their journey was leisurely and uneventful. A week later, Cape Fear, Myrtle Beach and Folly Beach to the south of Charleston were behind them, and on October first they were feeding at a quiet estuary south of Savannah. As usual, it was their custom to feed in the early morning, then meander southward during the day, stopping, when they so desired, to explore the dunes, flats and tidal creeks. If the evening tide was low, they preferred sandbars and tidal flats for roosting, but on those nights when the tide was full, they retreated reluctantly to the sand dune thickets.

Each evening Tara's parents pointed out to her the unending journey of Arcas around Polaris, and also the apparently continual descent of the constellation and the polar star toward the horizon.

Near Mayport, along one of the most deserted stretches of beach on the Atlantic coast, they paused one evening to roost comfortably on an odd outcropping of rocks. The angle of Polaris above the horizon, as always, mirrored that position on earth from which it was observed, at this point thirty degrees north latitude. As tiny as their brains were, they were able to calculate this position of Polaris which, without sophisticated instruments, man could not.

Man had determined (so they said) that they were instinctive creatures, incapable of reasoning, and motivated by their genes, hormones and external stimuli to perform by rote the actions of mating, brooding of the eggs and chicks, the feeding of their young and the prompting of them to fly.

But who can explain those mysterious actions that are locked within the deep recesses of their diminutive brains: the ability to tell time, to measure the distance the sun travels along the horizon, or to measure the angle of the sun above it? Why do they mate for life? Why are they so caring for those who are sick or injured? There are too many questions without answers to pass them off as insignificant bits of life which have no meaning to us. For if we cannot relate to them, how can we relate to ourselves?

The days passed and their southward migration continued: Cocoa Beach, then Key Largo. Here, Tara saw for the first time, over the salt marshes of the Florida Keys, a snowy-white egret in lazy flight, and a glossy ibis, its bronze plumage gleaming in the bright sun as it alternated its flying with languid periods of gliding.

The northern coast of Cuba was their next stop and they rested here for a few days before flying over the Guantanamo Naval Base and the Windward Passage to the westernmost tip of Haiti. The final and most strenuous test for Tara came three days later when her parents guided her south-southeast on the final leg of their journey, four hundred miles across the Caribbean Sea to the salt-white sands of Aruba where they would pass the winter in peaceful relaxation.

CHAPTER IV

Tara would not feel the urge to breed until the spring of her fourth year. In the meantime, changes would take place within her body, and events would occur in her young life which would flow naturally toward her forthcoming maturity. During this carefree interval, she would, for the only time in her existence, be able to pause and smell the flowers.

Her parents remained with her throughout the first winter, during which time she learned of the best feeding areas on Aruba and along the northern coast of Venezuela. She was also taught to avoid those areas where natives hunted her for food.

But then, as their prenuptial molt began in midwinter, the relationship between her and her parents began to change. The two adults were becoming more attentive to each other and were paying less attention to her. There was nothing unusual about this. They were simply following their instincts. They had brought forth new life, had nurtured it, had taught it how to survive, and had raised it to independence. They had been lucky, of course, as they had been meant to be. But now Tara was capable of taking care of herself; and if she hadn't been, it would have made no difference, for now the annual cyclic flow of hormones within her two parents was preparing them for the rigors of the approaching nesting season.

Tara, meanwhile, was spending more and more of her time with the other yearling terns, and when her parents began flying off by themselves for longer periods, and as their interest in her became less and less those few times they were in her vicinity, she was barely aware of this change in their attitude. Each night, though, at roosting time, she did manage to sleep nearby. The ties between parents and offspring must dissolve soon, as they were meant to do; but with Least Terns, the dissolution is gradual.

By early April when their prenuptial molt was completed, the yearling terns resembled their parents in both size and plumage. The white, black and yellow colors of the first year terns, however, were not quite as bright or as sharply defined as the older terns and this was to be expected.

By now Tara needed no urging to fix the position of the Little Bear and she did this each evening at the hour of eight. A few days later the adults started north with Tara and a few other yearlings trailing behind. Tara still recognized her parents, but it was at a discreet distance that she followed them northward and learned the way back to the home of her birth.

Many of the Least Terns did not nest as far north as Cape Cod, and by the time they reached Nauset Spit there were only ninety terns remaining out of an initial count of over three thousand. Many had returned to their nesting sites along the lower Atlantic coast, and over five hundred had bid adieu when they had reached Great Gull Island in Long Island Sound.

Tara, along with the other young terns, remained at the outer margins of the colony, watching without comprehension the strange courting antics of the adults. She could not relate to this simply because her ovary was not yet fully developed and would not be until her fourth year. Because of this immaturity, she and the other yearlings looked the other way and turned their attention to feeding and playing along the ocean beaches with young piping plovers whose parents were nesting in the same general area as the Least Terns.

It was a discouraging nesting season that spring and summer of nineteen seventy-four. All across the Cape, more nesting sites disappeared while predators ran rampant on the beaches. Tara was nearby when a few chicks hatched, but she and five other young Least Terns, along with some piping plovers, flew up the coast to Truro for a few weeks shortly thereafter.

They missed the disaster. Two beach buggies drove through the colony by mistake one day and the damage was done. Most of the chicks were killed, and those who did survive died of starvation when the adults deserted the colony to try elsewhere. When Tara returned, her parents were gone. If she ever did see them again, she would be unable to recognize them. She experienced no remorse about this, for it was merely another step dictated by her life cycle. So she resumed her random, jaunty lifestyle and flocked with the other yearlings until Arcas told her it was time to go.

She and the other young terns had no trouble reaching Aruba that autumn. And when she completed her prenuptial molt in late winter, she resemble closely an adult tern except that she was not yet sexually mature.

She returned again to Nauset Spit this third year of her life and was surprised and somewhat disappointed to find only five other Least Terns there. A day later when she flew over the territory of a mature male, he called to her. She landed nearby, her curiosity aroused, and was somewhat surprised and confused when he strutted over to her, walking stifflegged with his wings extended

Beach Buggy tracks at Nauset Spit

halfway. She cocked her head to one side and stared at him, somewhat perplexed. What is the matter with him? she asked herself. Why was he acting this way? But she waited expectantly, assuming he was only trying to be friendly and wanted to join her in a feeding foray at the inlet, or perhaps fly with her on an aimless journey along the Outer Beach.

She was startled, however, when he reached out and pecked her sharply on the shoulder. It was so dictated by nature that male and female terns must wear identical plumage and this was how he learned what sex she was. But she was not yet ready to understand this. If she had been a mature female ready to mate, she would have accepted this manner of questioning and not retaliated. But she didn't understand, so she pecked back at him and was surprised at the result. Instead of retreating, he rushed at her, thinking she was a male, and she instantly recognized his seriousness in defending his territory. She gave way without hesitation and flew a short distance away to a more serene atmosphere.

She was the only non-breeding Least Tern at the Spit that year, and she had no ties, so she decided to wander. For a few days she remained in the general vicinity of the Spit, eating when hungry and watching the courting terns from a distance. There was a larger colony of Common Terns near the fringes of the upper beach, and she was equally curious at the antics of both species. A few times she felt an urge to imitate them, not really knowing what she was doing. But she had no partner to accept her silverbait, and she was not interested in having another tern on her back. In addition, she could not understand why one bowed to the other who was strutting in circles; but she did give a halfhearted attempt to scrape a hole in the sand, not knowing why. From a distance she looked like an inexperienced breeder, but of course she was not.

Soon she tired of this and the next day she decided to move on. The month of April had been a dreary one on Cape Cod. The arrival of spring had been late and the damp, drizzly days had camouflaged the anxious flora which were waiting patiently for the warm days of May.

Tara had been chasing schools of small fish south of Nantucket when the weather changed. By the time she returned to the Spit, the warming rays from a bright golden sun were rewarding the ecosystem with triumphant colorful vistas of new flowery life. Tara saw the beginning of this from an altitude of five hundred feet. Cape Cod Bay gleamed bright and blue to the west, and when she saw the extensive flats shimmering in the distance she sensed correctly the presence of lush feeding grounds.

She flew effortlessly in their direction, her wings extending gracefully outward to their full span of twenty-one inches. She looked earthward, her tiny brown eyes focusing easily on the passing landscape. The kames of Eastham extend southwestward from the shore between Coast Guard Beach and Nauset Light. They are unlike the flat tablelands which extend northward into Wellfleet and Truro, but instead are made up of alternating hills and valleys. Red cedar trees dot the sinuous rolling hills which dip into and rise out of undulating grassy meadows. This combination continues without interruption until it reaches the Sandwich moraine in Orleans. Nauset Marsh graces its southeastern border while the Salt Pond Visitors Center sits proudly atop one of these hillocks.

She angled downward in a slow sweeping turn to the right. The sunlight blazed brightly on her silver-gray wings. Down below, a stone wall tumbled westward and was bordered by thickets of nannyberry bushed which were spraying their creamy-white flowers into the air like miniature water fountains. Along the roadsides violets sprinkled their light blue and lilac hues amongst the hardy weeds.

In the gardens and on the lawns, cultivated trees were in full flower. Wild cherry trumpeted the revival of spring, its clusters of white blossoms clothing it so heavily that its pale green leaves were barely visible. White-striped downy woodpeckers, the males sporting bright red patches on the backs of their heads, had deserted the back yard suet feeders and were now rapping away at the bark as they searched spiritedly for insect larvae. Crab apple trees were more demure, presenting their delicate white and red petals almost apologetically, while hawthorn trees were more boisterous, flaunting their fragrant crimson blossoms as brazenly as a firebush. A moment later, she circled low over a group of magnolia trees and caught the sweet scent of their white, pink and reddish blossoms sifting upward on warm, humid air. The large and glittery dark green leaves moved ever so slightly, as if bidding a gradious adieu.

She stayed in the vicinity of the Eastham flats for a few days before traveling northward. A few days later she was at the Massachusetts Audubon Sanctuary in Wellfleet and it so happened that she made this her home base for the remainder of the season.

By the time she reached the inlet of Hatch's Creek, most of the migrators had continued on their journey northward after touching down briefly to feed and rest. A few stragglers remained, however. Most numerous was a small flock of semipalmated sandpipers. She watched the small birds from a distance as they fed everywhere: on the mudflats at low tide, in the upper reaches of the ripening salt meadows, or running along the edge of a quiet surf. Then, a few days later, she noticed that the freckled-grayish birds with their white underparts and black legs were gone and she turned her attention to a pair of whimbrels which were resting for a few days on their pilgrimage to their nesting grounds on the western shore of Hudson Bay. The long-legged wading birds were using their long down-curved bills to feed on fiddler crabs at low tide near the rickety wooden bridge which one must cross to get to the beach from Goose Pond Trail. The trail runs along the upper reaches of the marsh before looping easterly into the upland country. Then at high tide she would watch wistfully when the two large brown birds with their blue-gray legs would fly to the drumlins in the marsh to rest.

But it was when she heard them call to each other with short, mellow whistles that she knew something was wrong. She shouldn't be alone, she thought. Where were the others of her kind? And the next morning, when dawn broke, rippling shades of lavender on high cirrus clouds, she watched the whimbrels with a benign curiosity when they headed northward, their long legs trailing gracefully behind. Then she was alone except for a large group of herring gulls and a smaller flock of black-backed gulls which her instinct told her to ignore.

The year was nineteen seventy-five and there were many things that she would never know. The number of Least Terns was down drastically all over the Cape, although there was some success at Nauset Heights and West Dennis Beach. But in the other areas predators, winged, four-legged and two-legged, took a frightful toll of eggs and chicks. She also would never know that under the most favorable conditions barely twenty percent of newborn Least Terns survive their first year, and that under the present conditions time was fast running out for them.

What she did know was that she was alone, but she could not understand why. The flocking instinct is strong in terns, and although she was able to feed easily at the estuary and to roost without fear in the drumlins at night, she continued to be uneasy. She spent much of her time soaring over Wellfleet Harbor, calling repeatedly in her high-pitched voice. At other times, when she was resting on the upper beach, she would experience an unexpected and unfathomable impulse to fly out over the water and then return. On other occasions, she would spot striped bass pursuing smaller fry through the cool green waters of the bay and would swoop low over them just to join in the excitement.

Then, a few days later, a small flight of young piping plovers flew into the sanctuary and landed by her side. They were a gregarious group, somewhat smaller than Tara, with white underparts and backs the color of dry sand. Although they had not yet reached maturity their legs and bills were yellow, while around their necks each sported a single dark, irregular band. When they were not feeding briskly on the mudflats at low tide or at the edge of the inrushing surf, their two-noted piping calls to each other floated across the dunes like airy notes from tiny organs.

They accepted Tara into their group without hesitation and for

the next few days her sense of loneliness dissipated. She was a beautiful, inspiring sight as she flew over the sanctuary, her joyous calls skimming across the swelling marsh like buoyant bits of gossamer. And when she flew among them, her long silvery wings and forked tail glinting in the sunlight, her superior flying talents made her stand out in sharp contrast to the plovers, whether they were skimming low across the shimmering dunes, or climbing high into a clear azure sky. She was most heavenly beautiful, however, in that splendorous instant of time when, just after landing, she extended her long, pointed, narrow wings high above her head and resembled a sacred archangel. Then she would fold them in close to her body and cross them scissors-like beyond her tail.

As the early days of June wore on, she became restless again, and began wandering further up the coast towards Blackfish Creek. The piping plovers willingly accompanied her, and each day in the late afternoon they returned to the sanctuary.

Their forays took them over dense woodlands where isolated horse chestnut trees were dressed in full glory, their silver blossoms opening elegantly in the warmth of the late spring sun. In these mixed forests, rufous-sided towees mingled together as their nesting season intensified. Blossoming huckleberry and scrub oak thickets concealed their nests and nestlings, while their drink-your-tea song rang out heartily through the pitch pine trees whose twigs were showing tiny nubs of new green growth. The white-bellied, rufous-sided, robin-sized birds with their white-spotted round tails and fire-red eyes scratched tirelessly for insects in the moist underlayer of the forest.

These secretive woodlands also sheltered wild lily-of-the-valley which boasted spikes of fine white flowers upon a single stem, while nearby, solomon's seal displayed paired, bell-shaped, greenish-yellow flowers hanging from their arched stems. Meanwhile, across the rolling heathland long interlacing vines of bearberry spread a thick carpet of small, shiny evergreen leaves while sprouting tiny white flowers. It was from this background that blue lupine chose to poke through with their nine-inch spikes and cap them victoriously with crowns of blue-violet flowers.

Then one day as she flew high over the upper limits of the marsh at Blackfish Creek, she looked in the direction of the Atlantic Ocean a bit longer than usual, and the Outer Beach tugged at her. She circled once more toward the southwest and the sanctuary. The piping plovers followed. Then she turned abruptly toward the east, calling over her shoulder at them to follow.

Ten minutes later they were over Marconi Beach, and when she saw the colony of Least Terns just beyond the limit of the last flood tide, she let out a screech of joy and dropped down amidst them. They accepted her with a casual indifference, however; but even so, she did spend a few days feeding with them while the plovers scampered hungrily along the edge of the surf.

A week later they crossed the Truro-Provincetown line and they spent the next two weeks mingling with those Least Terns nesting in the area. It was here for the first time that she saw the agonies and frustrations of the breeding season. Well over a hundred pair of Leasts were trying valiantly to bring forth new young. The struggle was desperate, however, because foxes, weasels and great horned owls were preying on them constantly while at Wood End, vehicles were driving through the colony.

Once again Tara was fortunate when she learned another valuable lesson. One evening two days after the beginning of summer, she was roosting in thick clumps of marram on a six foot row of secondary dunes. It was midnight and a full moon was riding low behind scattered low-flying clouds as it pulled the water steadily toward the upper beach. The terns continued to sit nervously on their nests but murmured apprehensively to each other as the tide approached its highest point.

Suddenly, Tara felt a faint vibration in her ears. Deep within her essence a vague memory formed of when she was a chick, and instinctively she crawled further into the thick beach grass and flattened herself as close to the ground as she could. The great horned owl flew out of the scrub pine forest, soared across the dunes on silent wings, and without warning was in the colony. Quickly she downed two chicks while the others scattered. Then she took a stubborn female which refused to leave the nest. She died instantly when the owl decapitated her. Then the predator flew back into the stunted forest to feed on its prize.

That was enough for Tara and the plovers. She would never forget that vague warning sign. They left Provincetown at dawn and reached the sanctuary in the early afternoon. She and the plovers continued to keep company with each other until early August when Arcas told her it was time to go. The plovers were not yet ready, so they parted reluctantly and she returned alone to the Spit at Nauset. It was deserted. She was still alone when she began her southward migration, but at Cuttyhunk she met a few other stragglers and they stayed together until they reached Aruba.

The Dunes

CHAPTER V

There was a predetermined characteristic within Tara which dictated that each spring she would spend three to four weeks migrating north to her nesting grounds on Cape Cod. Here she would mate and attempt to raise a family for approximately three or four months before returning to the Southern Hemisphere where she would winter for six months.

Once in her winter quarters (by the northern calendar, for it was actually summer in Venezuela) she had been embraced by a quiescent dormancy. Her autumn molt had created a winter plumage which had whispered softly of what her mood had been. From November to late January, her forehead, lores and crown had been as white as snow. Her crown, however, had been laced boldly with black shaft lines. The back of her head and nape had been a dusky gray and had been connected to her eye by a narrow streak. Her hindneck had been as white as her forehead while her mantle had become a darker gray than it had been in summer. Meanwhile, the leading edge of her inner wing and forearm had turned a grayish-black while the majority of her primaries had become a dull slate-gray.

Tara, like all living creatures, was instinctively responsive to forces over which she had no control. She was, in some ways, more fortunate than other forms of life. Her entire life cycle was governed by two "clocks," one biological, the other celestial. The two of them meshed smoothly and guided her mysteriously through the seasons of her life while the lessons she had learned first from her parents and then by herself gave her the necessary tools she needed to survive and reproduce.

Her biological clock was sensitive to light. The tilt of the earth with its north pole pointing towards the north star is responsible for the incessant progression from season to season which is so intimately associated with the cyclic variation in the length of daylight. And although this variation is slight on the northern coast of Venezuela, it is enough to influence Tara's biological clock.

Following the completion of her autumn molt, she had lived in a quiet, serene interlude with others of her species. In addition, hundreds of Common Terns along with a few Roseate Terns had shared this section of Venezuela.

Then, in late January, as she approached her first breeding season, the gradually increasing length of daylight began to exert a subtle effect on her hypothalamus. The increasing amounts of ultraviolet light were prompting it to send signals to the anterior pituitary gland which was responding by stepping up its secretion of thyrotropic and gonadotropic hormones. These two hormones in turn were causing an increased cell activity in their respective target organs.

Her ovary, under the influence of gonadotropin, began enlarging in early February. Actually, she had two ovaries, but as it was in all forms of bird life, her right ovary had atrophied and was nonfunctioning. Her left ovary, which was located near her backbone, was enlarging for the first time and was beginning to secrete the gonadal hormones which would prepare her for her first attempt at reproduction. These vague beginnings would increase steadily all through spring and into migration, then peak out shortly after her arrival at Nauset Spit.

As the flow of these hormones had increased all through February, changes had come about in Tara. Her prenuptial molt was in its final stages and she had acquired the distinctive plumage of the breeding Least Tern.

And what a beautiful creature she had become. She was the most delicate, almost fragile-appearing bird of the eastern coast. She was robin-size, which made her the tiniest and daintiest of her genus. She was no more than eight or nine inches long, while her twenty-one inch wing span was scarcely two thirds that of the Common Tern. But strangely enough, these dainty, tapering wings gave her a light, graceful flight which contrasted sharply with her shrill, piercing calls.

Her crown was now a glossy black and a narrow white crescent with horns on each side extended from above her eyes to her bright yellow, black-tipped bill and was separated from her white cheek by a dusky line which ran through her eye.

Meanwhile, the entire upper portion of her body including her forked tail had turned a lustrous, pale grayish-blue. This distinctive coloration, however, ended sharply at the base of her black cap and, beginning at the junctions of her neck and sides of her head, faded gradually into the satiny, pure white of her underparts. Her two outer primaries, reaching out from each wrist, had turned black with a white space on their inner webs, while the remainder of her primaries had become a darker shade of gray than her mantle. Finally, her legs and feet had turned a bright orange-yellow.

As these transitions were taking place, the other hormone produced by the anterior pituitary gland, thyrotropin, was exerting its prompting powers. At a leisurely rate the hormone persuaded Tara's thyroid gland to generate increasing amounts of thyroidal hormone. And as it did so, her appetite strengthened and she began laying down considerable amounts of fat deposits. In addition to all of this, her disposition was changing.

From November through January, she had, as had others of her species and genus, been subdued, introspective and reflective. And although she had not experienced the excitement, nervousness and agitation of the prior nesting season, she had followed the others into this mellow, quiescent and restful stage of their annual cycle.

But now the tempo of her arena had changed. It was the second week in March and preparations for the northward migration were taking place. On the plains of Cuba, in the stunted undergrowth of Mexico, within the rain forests of the Yucatan Peninsula, and along the coasts of Central and South America, a mystic restlessness was taking place. The birds of North America must soon be leaving for their breeding grounds.

Tara, like the others, was no longer indifferent. This was her first experience with the preliminaries of the breeding phase of her life cycle and she was having difficulty understanding her feelings and actions. As the days of March waned she became more restless, more easily agitated. She took on a more aggressive attitude in her search for food as she mingled with the other Least, Common and Roseate Terns. Also, she was calling more often when she and the other terns chased each other across the muddy sand flats and estuaries.

A few days later she sensed a change in her surroundings. Then she realized that half the flock had disappeared. She did not know that many of the males had gone on ahead to claim their piece of breeding territory. A few mated pairs still lingered, but gradually they slipped away and left the dwindling flock.

Tara watched them leave with an increasing uneasiness but nevertheless she continued to gorge herself on the endless supply of silverbait. Each night she fixed the position of Arcas standing twelve degrees above the northern horizon. And each night the cup inched further upward reaching slowly for that position which was imprinted on her meager brain. And as it neared that position, shadowy visions of Nauset Spit, Monomoy, Lewis Bay, Nobska Light and Cuttyhunk floated dreamily across her subconscious and each night the visions became sharper, brighter and more colorful like an instant snapshot developing in bright sunlight before human eyes.

Then, at the end of the first week in April, her visions of Cape Cod reached their maximum intensity, Arcas raised her silent voice, called across light-years of time to her, and she knew.

The next day she was gone.

The Spit

CHAPTER VI

It was late afternoon when she reached the inlet. She was tired and her flight feathers were tattered from the long migration even though she had stopped and rested each evening. The journey had been uneventful until she had reached Virginia Beach. Then a heavy fog had rolled into the area and she had been grounded for three days. She had been aggravated and confused by this. Twice in desperation she had broken through the cloud cover into bright sunlight, but when she had been unable to see the coastline to get her bearings, she had returned reluctantly to earth calling out angrily in frustration.

Finally, when the fog lifted on the third evening, Arcas peeked through the thinning clouds and told her she was behind schedule. The next day she flew steadily until she reached Montauk Light. She had no interest in the Least Terns from Great Gull Island which were roaming around the area, and instead fed by herself in a quiet estuary before roosting uneasily at the tip of a long breakwater. She was off again at dawn and flew nonstop to the marsh in Centerville where she rested for a few hours before undertaking the final flight to the inlet.

Now she was home. Although she scanned the area nervously with tiny brown eyes, she was uninterested in the familiar surroundings. This was her first breeding season. She was a full-fledged adult and her genes and reproductive hormones were telling her that it was time to find a mate. But before that, she must replenish her depleted fat reserves and regain her strength.

She was alone no longer. The inlet was teeming with Common, Roseate, Arctic and Least Terns. Most of the Least Terns along with a few of the others were from the southern side of the inlet at Nauset Heights Beach. They were fortunate. The well-posted area was difficult for the public to get to and was patrolled by concerned citizens whose attitude was more educational than police-like. However, to the north New Island, which had once been the eroding tip of Nauset Spit, was the breeding home for over four hundred pair of Common Terns and a much lesser number of Roseate Terns. But these colonies were not where she was destined to be. She did not know why, but deep within her instinctive brain, she knew she should be at the Spit.

For the next few days, she and the other terns concentrated on their feeding. And for the first time she noticed that although she and the other Leasts fed primarily in the shallows and tidal creeks, the Common, Roseate and Arctic Terns fed farther out in the deeper littoral waters.

Then, as she became well-fed, changes began taking place in her manner. First she became more aware of the other terns and their actions. The terns from opposite sides of the inlet associated freely with each other at feeding time and she was overjoyed when she frolicked excitedly with the other Leasts. Each evening, though, they retreated to their colony at Nauset Heights and although she roosted with them for a few nights, she felt uncomfortable. Each day she returned to the Spit hoping to find others of her species, and each day she was disappointed.

As the passing days produced an increasing amount of daylight, her hormonal activity continued to intensify, while within her ovary two ova moved closer and closer to maturation. But there were other visual stimuli affecting her.

On New Island, Common Terns were just a few days away from copulation. Their vivid black caps extended to the lower level of their dark brown eyes while their pearly-blue mantles deepened in color until they ended abruptly at their snow-white rumps.

Tara flew among them for a short distance while they passed minnows back and forth between their vermillion-colored, black-tipped bills. Then, when they returned to the beach, circling each other on coral-red feet and displaying their grayish-black to grayish-blue primaries and secondaries, she felt an increase in her own sexual excitement.

At Nauset Heights she searched frantically for attention among the Leasts but was ignored. They were all mated as were the black-billed Roseate Terns whose breasts seemed to be blushing with a procreative passion as they courted in the thickets of flowering beach pea in the upper dunes.

As the end of May approached, the young virgin Tara was rapidly reaching the apex of her desire to reproduce. Just watching the courtship antics of the other terns produced an increased activity of her anterior pituitary gland which in turn caused an even greater outpouring of reproductive hormones by her swollen ovary. She was caught up now in the enchantment of reproduction. Copulation was occurring continually among the terns, eggs were being laid and mated pairs were settling down to the business of brooding.

Rapidly, now, the terneries developed the traditional patterns for which they are so well-known. These exquisite, naive birds of the beaches had scratched shallow craters in the sand with no attempt at concealment (except for the Roseate Terns which somehow know they had a better chance in the upper dune hollows where there was thicker vegetation).

Noted for many different behavioral aspects, one standout was their sociability which was manifested by their habit of resting in flocks along the sandy beaches near the edge of the foaming surf; by the way they fed in loose, noisy parties at the generous inlets and estuaries, caught flying insects over the cool, moist marshes or dove into the warming waters off the Outer Beach for silverbait, killifish, sand eels or minnows. In addition, their continual movement in and about the colony was distinctive as the various species intermingled in an apparent mass of confusion, calling back and forth to each other with their shrill, sharp cries. And finally, their nervous excitability was also demonstrated by sudden, unexplained flights out over the water before returning and settling down with their incessant, clamorous chattering.

Tara was becoming frantic. Unable to understand her frustration, she began executing generic patterns which were as awkward as they were mystifying. Many times she offered fish or shrimp to another Least, expecting to have it returned to her. And when it was not, she would anger and attack the offender as she substituted fighting for courtship. It was difficult for her to sleep at night and each morning after feeding, she could be seen at the Spit alone, bowing to her invisible suitor or turning counterclockwise with drooping wings and making shallow scrapes in the warm sand.

Then one morning her life changed. She awoke in a thick fog which blanketed the Lower Cape from Chatham to Wellfleet. She wandered down to Pleasant Bay for a few hours, waiting patiently for the fog to lift, and reconnoitered Tern Island which was now deserted by its namesakes. A few hours later as the gray mist began lifting over the clammy barrier beaches and marshes, she retraced her route back to the Spit. Her flight was a lackadaisical and haphazard one, almost as if she was attempting to feign disinterest in her plight. She halted for a short time at the Nauset Heights colony and as usual she was ignored by the mated pairs and non-breeding terns. A short time later she dallied over the dripping marsh for a few moments, dipping and rising as effortlessly as a butterfly in a gusty autumn breeze.

Then she saw them. She could hardly believe it when she saw the ten Least Terns. She had no way of knowing that their primary nesting site at Gray's Beach in Yarmouth had been molested by a pair of great horned owls. The owls had taken two females that frightful night while the other terns had scattered. What Tara saw was four mated pairs and two widowed males. There was also a mated pair of Arctic Terns which had arrived independently of the Least Terns. They had not been comfortable at Marconi Beach and had drifted southward until they had found a more gravelly area at the Spit. Now, as Tara warily circled above the scene, the Arctic Terns renewed their courtship ritual. Curious now, she joined the tiny colony, and for two days both species flew back and forth across the Spit in airy flights. Then, the urge to mate which had been swept away by the terror of that night returned to the mated Least Terns, and she watched their courtship actions with a deep, seething anticipation.

Soon, she found this too frustrating and she turned her attentions to the two males. One was older than she, perhaps seven, and a trifle larger, while the other one was younger, about the same age as she. Both had staked out their territory and now whenever Tara circled above them they each called to her, lifting their voices in high-pitched sexual calls. It was the older one which drew her down. His name was Timbre.

The mid-morning sun was dispersing the heavy fog from the marsh which bordered the westerly side of the Spit, while four-foot waves were breaking lethargically against its ocean side. She could wait no longer. But just as she was about to answer his call, the younger male intercepted her. He flew alongside with a shrimp in his bill, enticing her with low, persuasive calls. Then, as she reached for the offering, Timbre rose quickly from the beach and challenged him, his bill pecking viciously at the underpart of his wing. Quickly, the younger tern dove earthward with Timbre following doggedly at his tail. Once on the ground they struggled briefly, bills locked together as they rolled over and over on the gravelly sand. Soon the younger one sensed the stronger determination and power of Timbre. He decided that discretion was the better part of valor, and yielded. A moment later, when Timbre rushed at him again, he flew away hoping to find a more hospitable atmosphere to the north.

Tara had watched the struggle from a distance. When it was over, she realized that she was alone with him, the other mated pairs busy with their partners. She landed lightly in his territory and eyed him cautiously from a discreet distance. Instinctive forces were coming into play now. She waited. He was just as wary, but he edged closer to her. A vision of his former mate drifted hazily through his scanty memory and intensified his excitement. His testes had increased over two hundred times in size and the frustration of not being mated was being expressed by his aggressiveness. Yet, he sensed this tern was a young one and he wasn't sure of its gender. He approached Tara with a strutting, almost bombastic gait, unaware of his actions.

In the meantime, her emotions were mixed. She was unafraid, yet she sensed this was not the time to be belligerent. Timbre came closer, speaking to her in subdued clucks. She answered him in the same tone as she took one step backward. He knew he must peck at her, but somehow sensed it should not be too harsh. He did not want to scare her away. He reached over and pecked her lightly on the shoulder. She took another step backward and bowed her head. He pecked at her again, a trifle harder this time, and again she backed away. Her eyes never left his. He continued to stare at her for a few moments. Then, suddenly, he flew away towards the inlet. She waited patiently, smoothing her shoulder feathers with her bill where he had pecked her.

Ordinarily, she would have gone with him, but these were not ordinary times. Vaguely she remembered watching first encounters like this before, and by some mysterious means, her intuition told her to remain in his territory. She was somewhat flustered and apprehensive, and she telegraphed this by hopping about and fluttering her primaries. Instinctively, she commenced preening herself, hoping this would calm her nerves. Deftly she reached above and across her wing to the small oil gland situated just below her tail and placed a small drop on her bill. Then she drew a few secondary flight feathers through her bill, making sure the oil touched all of the webbing. She repeated the process a few times, pausing now and then to survey the Spit.

It was warming quickly and would be a slightly hazy day, the plodding fishing boats barely visible beyond the shoals. The Spit was deserted except for the Least Terns and the one pair of Arctic Terns. A mile northward, however, beach lovers and surfers were beginning to congregate on Coast Guard Beach. She would forever have difficulty in comprehending this form of life with which she was forced to share the beach.

She turned her attention back to the terns and viewed their actions with an increasing interest. Two pair had already copulated, as had the Arctic Terns, and the females were preparing to lay. The female of another pair had already dropped her eggs, while the fourth pair were in the final stages of courtship, maneuvering and waiting for the right moment to copulate. Their calls resounded across the Spit as they chattered back and forth with the males leaving for short periods of time to fish for food.

After a few moments she became concerned. Where was he? What was taking him so long? She began fluttering about a bit, flexing her wings as she hopped and flew short distances. Then she began calling in high "ki-ki-ki-ki" sounds, her bright yellow, black-tipped bill wide open as she stretched her neck toward the inlet. Then she saw him. He was a hundred feet above the dunes, dancing through the air while he executed short banking turns, first to the right, then to the left. He held a small sand eel in his bill and he was calling happily to her as the distance between them narrowed.

The pitch of his call slid lower and became more slurred as he side-slipped toward her for a moment. Then he recovered quickly and reached for the sky, his long, silvery wings taking deep bites out of the humid air. She was in the air quickly, gaining ground on him easily as he followed the foaming surf northward. When she caught up with him, he passed the sand eel to her, and as the wind whistled gloriously past their ears, she could just hear the low, sensual clucks emanating from his throat. She was stimulated by his tone and instinctively she understood its meaning. For the next thirty minutes they darted and flashed across the area. Once they went as far as Nauset Light, circling it like it was a pylon. And twice they swept out across the water for a few hundred yards, dipping and rising between the crests of the shallow waves, calling to each other with their high-pitched voices when the distance between them increased, then lowering their voices to sepulchral, intimate calls when they flew close enough to each other to pass the sand eel back and forth. Then, just before returning to the Spit, they swooped low over the flowering marsh and showed the nesting red-winged blackbirds how to catch flying insects.

She followed him back to the territory. Once on the ground, he turned to face her. The sand eel was clasped firmly in his bill and he knew he was about to meet the final test. He stepped toward her and offered the sand eel. She decided to be coy and turned her head away. He shifted the sand eel in his bill and offered it again. She turned her back to him but watched him slyly from the corner of her eye. He was agitated now and becoming angry. He called twice, hopping up and down as he came around to face her again. She had irritated him long enough. She had the sand eel in her bill before he realized it and swallowed it in one gulp. At this gesture he stepped closer to her and their bills crossed scissor-like. She murmured to him softly and bowed her head. He stroked his bill lovingly along her white forehead and their pact was sealed.

For the next three days they were inseparable. Whether feeding at the inlet, or roosting on the upper beach, or flying over the shoreline that was becoming more crowded each passing day with tourists and vehicles, they never parted. The two lovers became primarily absorbed in a devout courtship, which flowed easily into a predetermined and passionate cycle leading to reproduction. Each step along the way to copulation brought about an increased activity of the anterior pituitary gland. And the anterior pituitary in return intensified their courtship ritual.

It was mid-June now, and the other terns were incubating their eggs while the males provided food. Gradually, Tara and Timbre spent more time on the ground in their territory. He was becoming more aggressive as his desire increased, and she was unable to resist his attentions. She was still unsure of herself, but instinctively she followed his lead knowing somehow that she could trust him and

Nauset Light

that he would lead her into an infinite climax which would finally satiate that mysterious and perplexing unknown force that had been tormenting her since February.

He began strutting before her, walking stiff-legged, tail spiked high in the air, neck stretched skyward, wings partly open, their tips barely touching the ground. She watched him warily as he circled her, but she kept turning with him, her head bowed submissively, her snow-white breast just touching the warm sand.

These actions continued for two days. His were repetitious, of course, maneuvers he had performed many times before, while hers were generic, those she had inherited, now being put to the test for the first time. They were instinctive actions whose source was in their genes, actions they performed without knowing why. Before long, she sensed she should allow him to get behind her. He was talking to her gently in seductive tones, trying to reassure her.

While these preliminary ongoings continued, their purpose was fast approaching. Their effect on the interplay between her hormones and ovary reached its climax in the early afternoon when the two ova broke through the surface of the ovary and entered the oviduct. It was the slight twinge of pain in her abdomen that prompted her next inherited move. She turned her back to him, breast bowed, tail spiked high in the air, and glanced apprehensively over her shoulder at him. She was uneasy and confused, caught up in the mixed conflicts of the unknown versus her natural instincts. At the sight of her raised tail and inviting cloaca, his passion crested and quickly he was on her back. But this was new to her and she just as quickly shook him off. But again she presented the copulatory position to him, not knowing why. Twice more he mounted her and twice more she shook him off. But he persisted, calling loudly as their aphrodisia reached its zenith. The next time, she was ready. Their cloacas touched, then locked, and for a few brief moments millions of spermatozoa poured out of him and into her. Then their fleeting physical union was over, but it would signal the beginning of a hallowed liaison which would end only with the death of one of them.

Their mood changed. For the next twenty-four hours while the fertilized eggs underwent their journey to the outside, Tara turned her attention to the nest. She fussed about it like the apprehensive mother she would soon become. It was no more than a shallow, saucer-like depression, but the instinctive forces governing her behavior could not be changed. And why should they? For thousands of years they had been passed along from generation to generation. With some minor variations, of course. All the terns migrated when Polaris and Arcas told them to, but their generic imprinting varied, and because of this the migratory call came at different times and guided them to different latitudes all along the

Atlantic seaboard. They would always attempt mating at their primary nesting site, but when these efforts were frustrated, as they often were, their reproductive hunger would overcome their generic imprinting and forced them to seek out the next most desirous alternative breeding spot.

And so it was that the intense desire to copulate had been intimately connected with her scrapes in the sand. Now her instincts took on a different tone, as did his. It was time to prepare the nest, and she had no time to feed. Busily she searched for pebbles, bits of shell, small pieces of seaweed, anything to line the nest with and make it appear like anything but what it was. Camouflage was needed, as much as possible. He, of course, knew what she was up to, and made sure that she was well-fed. She was in and out of the nest all of that day, first placing a piece of shell, then hopping a short distance away to look at it while cocking her head from side to side, clucking to herself in an admonishing tone, returning to reposition the shell, accepting a shrimp from Timbre, then settling upon the nest as if brooding.

He accepted her sudden indifference, understanding its reasons and knowing this was how it should be. During their first night together as partners they roosted near the nest under a cloudless sky and kept their ears tuned for unfamiliar sounds. They took turns sleeping, their bodies touching like lovers, and from time to time the one awake would reach over with its bill and stroke the neck of the sleeping one. As the nighttime hours ebbed, and as a salmon-colored sky trumpeted the arrival of dawn, she felt a slight discomfort in her lower abdomen and settled determinedly into the nest. He sat next to her for a few moments while they watched the orange fireball climb quickly over the horizon. Then, as the day brightened, he became restless. For the next eight hours, their actions took different directions. While she sat doggedly on the nest, rising from time to time to change position, he was a bundle of nerves; fishing at the inlet, feeding her until she refused any more, flitting about, calling to the other terns. Finally, near noontime, he settled down and sat next to her, enjoying the heat of the day and watching the thick stalks of cord grass bending slightly in the mild late-spring breeze.

At midafternoon she reached over, stroked his neck with her bright yellow bill and spoke to him in a muted tone. She could feel the egg coming and she wanted to be alone. A moment later he was off and heading for the inlet to fish.

A few moments following his departure she experienced some discomfort as the egg began pushing through her cloaca to the outside. She pushed firmly against it with her cloacal muscles, breathed a whispery cry of pain, then felt the egg leave her body. She stepped out of the nest and looked down. The inch-long egg was sand-colored with some irregular dark spots. She touched it hesitantly with her bill and it rolled over a half turn. She looked skyward, wishing he would return so she could share this moment with him. A few moments later, he did. She waited patiently for his approval which he shouted shrilly. Then he gave her the killifish.

She laid the second egg a day later and they settled into the routine of brooding. For seventeen days and nights they incubated the eggs. Each day she could be seen sitting devotedly. It was her habit to sit facing the wind, no matter what strength it was, and she was a picture of serenity as she brooded with her head held high and her wings criss-crossed over her deeply forked tail. Their roles complemented each other perfectly. While she was content to sit placidly, Timbre flitted nervously about the barrier beach. He fed her constantly, so much so that often she had to refuse his offerings and instead exhort him to eat with muted, twittering calls. He was undaunted by all of this, and time passed swiftly for them as she followed his movements with a benign but loving interest.

Each afternoon he relieved her, and dutifully but impatiently he took his turn brooding the eggs while she bathed in the breakers. She was a picture of enchantment as she splashed playfully in the salty water. Then, with a boisterous whirring of her wings and tail, she would dry herself off before leaving for the inlet where she would satisfy her flocking instinct by mixing with the other terns. But it would not be long before she would remember Timbre and the eggs, and she would return to the nest to resume her incubating duties.

Their routine varied little, but the weather did. Most of the days began with a damp, gray, lingering fog which hung over the barrier beach like the low-lying cloud it was. Most days it would burn off by mid-morning, but a few times it was a prelude to one of those dreary, drizzly days which the Cape does not care to admit to, and which dampens the enthusiasm of the tourists for any outdoor activities. Only the determined sport fisherman relishes that kind of weather. Twice, torrential rain showers swept across the Spit from the southwest and drenched the colony. And it was on those days that the vibrant floral colors of late spring retreated within themselves temporarily and waited for the brilliant streams of sunlight to burst through the cloud cover and revive their sumptuous display.

The vagaries of the weather, however, did not disturb Tara or Timbre or the rest of the colony. Neither the heat of a midday burning sun, pouring rains, nor thunderous bolts of lightning disturbed them. It was the skunks that ravaged them. Timbre saw them first.

It was an hour after midnight and a few thin, scattered, low-flying clouds streamed past a low-riding, almost full moon which

Tara on the nest

had coaxed an abnormally high tide to its highest limit. Bright moonlight bathed the barrier beach and rippled long shadows of dunes along their seaward sloping sides bordering the colony. Blades of beach grass bowed and waved limply while their shadows followed in quiescent obedience. Nauset Light skimmed its flashing beacon in eerie silence across the shore and out to sea. Even the surf was hushed, four foot breakers foaming luminously on the descending foreshore and spewing silvery spheres of spray skyward where fleetingly they glittered in the moonlight before returning from whence they came. Behind the beach, the marsh was still, the lush, coiling tidal creeks almost overflowing as the high tide flooded across the acres of cordgrass and salt hay.

Timbre spotted the two skunks coming down the beach single file and quickly roused Tara. He led her away from the nest, and although she was reluctant to follow, she did so unhesitatingly and without question. Timbre knew that their best chance to save the eggs was to get as far away from the nest as possible and hope that the skunks would not find it. Then they awoke the other terns, exhorting them with "whuit-whuit-whuit" calls. They chose, however, to remain and face the challenge. But to no avail. The skunks calmly and deliberately ate their way through the colony, devouring all the eggs. Tara and Timbre were fortunate. Their nest was on the outer periphery of the colony, near the base of the dunes, and the skunks failed to find it.

The loud, angry cries of Tara, Timbre and the other terns as they harassed the marauding skunks roused the New Island colony which in turn alarmed the colony across the inlet at Nauset Heights. It was two hours before they all settled down again. The next morning the grieving terns were gone and Tara and Timbre were alone for the remainder of the season.

The summer passed with only one other distraction. Their two chicks hatched a few days following the invasion of the skunks and Timbre worked himself into near-exhaustion in his efforts to keep them well-fed. They were fortunate that he did not have to travel far to harvest the tiny minnows which this season were extremely plentiful in the shallow tidal pools. And in the late afternoon of each day he would plop down wearily to take his turn brooding the two young ones. He was amazed at how much they grew in each twenty-four hour period, and when he covered their tiny, quivering bodies lightly with each wing, even his small brain capacity was capable of knowing the satisfaction of caring for new life. How often, he would ask himself, did she call up to him lightly for more food, and how many times did he pass her a shrimp or a minnow while a screeching, gaping mouth pushed out hungrily from beneath her wings?

As usual the chicks grew rapidly and within a few days they

were scampering about the beach, each day moving farther afield from the nest and into the protective clumps of beach grass, or splashing about in the last gasps of the incoming breakers. Tara and Timbre were not aware that their territory was well-posted and that they presented a visual feast for those who watched from a distance through field glasses. Meanwhile, the two parents dutifully oversaw the antics of the chicks as they progressed steadily toward the fledgling stage. Only once were they threatened, or thought they were.

The marsh hawk and its mate had been nesting in the thick vegetation behind the old Coast Guard Station since May. It was then that the shadbush had announced the triumphant return of spring by blossoming first with its cloak of tiny white flowers and then pushing forth its cinerous-green leaves. Blackberry, highbush blueberry and dwarf sumac had become interwoven with bullbrier, while nearby, beach plum bushes had exploded with pinky-white blossoms. Beyond the thicket, slender, cone-shaped red-cedar trees dotted the rolling hills along with a few medium-sized glacier erratics. The hawks' nest had been built on the ground in a natural hollowed-out opening of the thicket, and here they could raise their chicks in safety. Now, two months later, the male was quartering low over the marsh.

The marsh had not been in existence very long. Actually, it was quite young compared with others on Cape Cod and along the Atlantic seaboard. When Champlain had sailed into the inlet in sixteen hundred and five, the harbor had consisted of channels bordered by shoals and sand banks, and had been deeper that it is now. But behind the ever-growing barrier beach where the tide had covered and uncovered the flats twice each day, the marsh had had its beginning. Like Champlain, cord grass had been the pioneer. It is unable to grow when constantly immersed in salt water like eel grass, but rather thrives best when its root system is covered for twelve hours each day. When these conditions are met, shoots of this hardy broad-leafed grass appear, and mature into rigid, unbending stalks up to six feet tall. As the years pass, the underground root system multiplies and fans out across the lower limits of the infant marsh. Each year the grass dies and adds its decaying blades to the silt, sand and clay brought in on the high tides and trapped by the root system. Season follows season, generation follows generation, while fresh clumps of cord grass appear, keeping pace with the rising peaty hummocks. As the tides etch fresh channels among these hummocks, new colonies of cord grass line their edges. These happenings continue for lifetimes while dead, decaying organic matter along with silt introduced into the enlarging marsh from fresh water streams flowing into it from the upland country add their contribution. Eventually, the marsh is built up to a level where the high tides can no longer cover it, and it is here where cord grass ceases to grow.

If cord grass is the pioneer, then salt hay is the homesteader. It is in the great expanse of the inner marsh, which is covered only twice each month by the full and new moon tides, that this salt meadow grass flourishes. This is the shorter, finer grass which builds up the inner marsh until a dynamic equilibrium is reached. It is the grass which Cape Cod farmers used to harvest each summer for their livestock, or to use as thatch for their roofs, or to mound around their foundations in winter to keep out the cold. And finally, it is the grass that is flattened down by the blowing winds to form curling cowlicks.

Spike grass is a common companion of salt hay, although it is shorter and much finer. At the outer limits of the marsh, the presence of dark green, black grass indicates the availability of fresh water. Glasswort, saltwort and other salt-tolerant plants trim the edges of the marsh and dot the hummocks along with late-flowering marsh rosemary or sea lavender.

But why a salt marsh? What is the significance of their contribution to the environment and why should they be allowed to survive? For a number of reasons. One is that acre for acre they are more productive than hay, wheat or corn fields. Only sugar cane surpasses them. And a salt marsh needs no fertilization. The decaying vegetation is acted upon by bacteria and fungi to produce detritus, which functions as nourishment for both the vegetation and the primary consumers. It is the grasses which are the producers that give up their energy to the consumers. It goes without saying, of course, that the first line of consumers will be eaten by the second line of consumers which in turn will be eaten by the third line of consumers, and so on up the food chain ladder. This interlocking network of grass, bacteria, fungi, insects, snails, crabs, fish, birds and mammals yields from five to ten tons of food each year. Slightly more than half of this rich mixture is consumed by the marsh flora and fauna while the rest is carried down to the sea by tides.Without this surplus the productivity of the fish and shellfish industry would be drastically reduced along the North American coast. Without the salt marsh, the Atlantic flyway of southward-migrating shorebirds would pass into history along with the birds, as would those that use them as winter feeding grounds.

In addition, many of those who have dredged or filled marshes in order to construct marinas or recreational waterfront property have discovered much to their anguish that a salt marsh is a natural, protective buffer zone between land and sea. Not only do they lessen the impact of fierce storm waves which periodically pummel the coast, but they also act as a sponge, soaking up the abnormal flood tides while protecting the higher ground.

So, the hawk was soaring over a marsh, the existence of which was no longer tenuous because it was within the borders of the Cape Cod National Seashore. It had not been one of the one-third of Massachusetts salt marshes, or one-half of the Connecticut salt marshes which had been destroyed since nineteen hundred and forty-five. With varying percentages, the story has been the same along the remainder of the Atlantic coast.

But perhaps eventually it will become more and more recognized that a salt marsh is more useful alive than dead, that the preservation of one is a natural and inexpensive way to control erosion, that their esthetic beauty has more of a meaning than their multi-shades of green in summer or their flamboyant hues of gold and russet in the fall.

Tara and Timbre should not have feared the hawk that season, for the marsh had provided him and his family with a generous supply of moles, shrews and meadow and deer mice which lived in the tunnels beneath the wind-flattened, swirling cowlicks of salt hay. As usual his stomach was full, and he had no interest in the terns. His cinnamon-colored mate had taken their immature off for a flying lesson over Rock Harbor and he was alone to seek his own diversions. He quartered low along the edge of the marsh, tilting from side to side, his gray, narrow, forty-inch-long wings with their black-tipped primaries beating slowly, then gliding effortlessly with wings in an open V above the horizontal. Quite regularly his distinctive white rump would flash above his broad, barred, fan-shaped tail. Until it was time for him to be moving south, he was content to fly across his domain at a low altitude. But now that his chick was fledged, thoughts of migration began forming in his instinctive brain. During these migratory journeys he was prepared to seek out rising air currents, ride them as high as he could, then slip their grasp and soar until another thermal buoyed him upward again.

He had no interest in Tara, Timbre or their two chicks, and he ignored the two adults when they came flying in on his port quarter. They thought he was a threat and they pounced on him from both sides, wheeling and gyrating in close to him, and screaming ceaselessly as they lashed out at him. Still he paid little attention to them. He was searching for a thermal and was feathering the air delicately with his primaries, constantly adjusting them. In this way he varied the width of the slots between them in order to maintain stability. He turned away from the marsh and soared leisurely across the Spit, still ignoring Tara and Timbre who continued to dive at him repeatedly, closing within inches as their angry, high-pitched calls shattered the hot July day. A moment later, the outer limit of his right wing lifted suddenly and instinctively he turned to the starboard. Then the thermal grasped him, and quickly he was buoyed up and away from the terns, and his exhilaration was as strong as was the relief of Tara and Timbre as they turned away and returned to the two chicks.

Time passed quickly. The chicks were fledged the following week and a month later, in mid-August, Tara and Timbre were molting into their winter plumage. Goldenrod was in flower behind the dunes, while fleshy stems of glasswort were trimming the borders of the marsh with hues of salmon, crimson and rose. On the back side of the secondary dunes leaves of poison ivy, which in spring and summer had been a cucumber green, were just beginning to change color as they responded to the cooler, shorter days of late summer. Amongst all this, salt spray rose still scattered its modest pink blossoms, while clumps of beach grass were tiring from their difficult summer tasks. Within this mixed flora, the promise of beach plum in May, when it had laced the Spit with its pearly-white flowers, was evident, as its ripening, deep-red and purple fruit weighed heavily from its craggy branches.

Meanwhile, back in the heathlands, twelve- to eighteen-inch-high bushes of low, sweet blueberry were blooming with white and primrose-colored, urn-shaped flowers, and soon their deep blue and purplish-black berries would provide nourishment for late-migrating birds. In the meadows, the grass was tawny-colored now, and waving a sad good-bye to the southward-moving sun. Along the borders of the meadows, clusters of golden asters gleamed like miniature suns on foot-high stems which were thickly covered with fuzzy, gray-green leaves.

Once again the terns were feeling the urge to migrate as the Little Bear reached out into the northwest sky from its anchor, Polaris. It was now that Tara and her family joined up with the colony at Nauset Heights. The flocking instinct was upon them and, like the others, they spent a restless two weeks gorging themselves on killifish before beginning the long journey to Venezuela.

CHAPTER VII

That was the end of the happy times. For six more years their love sang a rhapsody across the sandy peninsula. A tragic rhapsody. A rhapsody of frustration. For six springs they raced the sun northward, guided by their stars. For six springs their genes called them back to their Spit. For six years they were together. And for six years their understanding of and devotion for each other reached limits unimaginable to those species with supposedly a higher level of intelligence.

One only had to watch the way they flew together, one instant a wing's-breadth away, followed by a momentary opening of the distance between them as they sought their own individuality by reaching into the endless blue of the firmament. One only had to hear them call to each other when fishing in the warming estuaries of the Atlantic coast while countless ocher-spreading dawns proclaimed countless rising suns. One only had to see them defend their territory when it was invaded by others, whether or not the intruders were of their own species. One only had to observe the way they loved each other. When mating, they orchestrated a symphony of sensuality as their reproductive actions developed a finesse and sophistication equal to the dance of the flowers. When not mating, they were just as attentive, only in a different way. One seldom saw the way they scissored beaks in sublime fidelity, or rubbed their necks together at dusk when sunset after sunset reflected broken ribbons of cadmium across tidal pools interlaced with soggy sandbars. Few ever saw the way they roosted. It made no difference whether they were resting on secluded barrier beaches, or on temporary sandbars, or on barnacle-encrusted jetties, or on the grassy drumlins of the inexorably disappearing marshes, it was their habit to roost neck to neck with their bodies facing in opposite directions.

It was during these peaceful hours when they would talk back and forth in throaty murmurs. On those evenings when the beach was still, when the rising moon laced a silvery lane of luminescence across the rippled sea, when the velvety onshore breeze whispered softly across the dunes and through the marram, when the comforting gurgling sounds in the tidal creeks drifted across the marsh and caressed their ears, this was when they asked each other—what was wrong? Where were the others? They asked this question of each other many times.

They asked it in the spring when the blossoming of red maple trees covered the awakening land with a deep, ruddy haze; when the weeping willows hung their long, graceful leaves from drooping branches which swung lazily at the edges of swamps and along shores of upland kettle ponds and streams; when the deciduous trees leaped from their winter repose and displayed their characteristic flowers and leaves—the silvery-green blossoms of the oak; the deep green, heavy-veined, saw-toothed leaves of the beech; and the white, sugary-scented flowers and feathery leaves of the locust.

They asked it while watching the nesters arrive and begin again their endless reproductive cycle. Tree swallows had returned in early April, a month before the terns. They had left their winter quarters in the Florida panhandle a few weeks earlier and had migrated up the coast feeding on bayberries. They do not feed exclusively on flying insects like other swallows of Cape Cod, and because of this they are able to move north earlier than the others. The sparrow-sized birds nested only in the boxes placed on poles in the back yards, fields and cranberry bogs. No longer were hollow tree cavities available for them. These original homes had disappeared more than a century ago when those trees, which had survived forest fires, had been cut down to be used as fuel for the Sandwich glass factory.

Now, as the warming days of April teased flying insects into the air, the tree swallows fanned out across the ponds, marshes and meadows, and satisfied their hunger. They were unmistakable as they flitted about, their shimmering green backs and snow-white undersides flashing boldly from dawn to dusk. Meanwhile, their fluid twitterings drifted over the greening moors while they alternated rapid strokes of their thin, pointed wings with short, undulating spurts of gliding. And it was when their brown-backed juvenals were fledged in late spring that Tara and Timbre looked on wistfully. And later, when spotted sandpipers with backs the color of burnt almond came bursting in from their winter quarters along the southern coast and began nesting in the dunes and along the tidal creeks, again they wondered with an uncomprehending melancholy, where were the others?

For six Junes, they watched the blooming of white rambling roses along weatherbeaten split rail fences, the almost apologetic appearance of tiny white flowers of sea-beach sandwort near the shore, and the edges of the upper marsh fill with long, willowy cattails. And for six years they watched sharp-tailed sparrows lay their greenish-white, brown-speckled eggs in nests made of seaweed and marsh grass. The broad orange triangle on their faces in combination with their unstreaked crowns was distinctive, and their barely audible trilling songs drifted lightly across the marsh as they constructed their nests amongst the stalks of salt hay. And once again

Tara and Timbre were forlorn when they watched both parents feed their demanding young.

For six years they tried courageously to bring forth new young to the fledgling stage, and for six years they failed. More than thirteen hundred pair of Least Terns returned to the Cape in nineteen hundred and seventy-seven. That was the year rats and weasels ran out of control through the South Cape Beach colony in Mashpee and the terns deserted it permanently. And at Provincetown the ever-increasing use of the beach by vehicles exerted so much pressure upon the terns that this was the year of their final attempt there.

When Tara and Timbre returned to the Spit that year, it was deserted. They stayed there for a few days, then reluctantly joined up with the colony at Nauset Heights. The choice was a difficult one, for their genes told them to breed at the Spit with the three hundred Commons and the few Arctics and Roseates, but their flocking instinct was stronger and they followed it. It was a difficult season for them. Perhaps it was the distraction of the unfamiliar colony, but whatever the reason, they scratched out their nest too far below the high tide line, and when an unexpectedly ferocious early June storm struck the shore on a neap tide, the water reached into the lower limits of the colony and washed away their eggs. When they tried to breed a second time, the outer limits of the colony were preyed upon by foxes. The constant uproar was too much for them and they abandoned any further efforts that year.

When they returned to the Spit in nineteen hundred and seventy-eight, they were one of only seven hundred pairs of Least Terns returning to the Cape. For a moment, they thought they had somehow miscalculated their position. The Spit looked nothing like it did the year before. They had no way of knowing of the Great Blizzard which had pummeled the Northeast in February. The storm had struck at the time of the new moon, and abnormally high tides in concert with thundering storm waves had battered the New England coast from Connecticut to Maine. The coast had suffered the most in those areas where man had come too close to the sea. It was here that the punishing heavy surf had broken through seawalls and had annihilated the efforts of those who had dared to challenge it.

But on Cape Cod, the purpose of natural barriers was demonstrated once again. Only at Provincetown, which had learned generations ago that from time to time it would have to pay a price for living so close to the sea, was damage severe. Once again it was the Great Outer Beach which had accepted the gauntlet, and its scarp had given ground grudgingly. But from Monomoy to Coast Guard Beach, it was the barrier beaches which had defended the fragile peninsula. The foredunes had taken the initial onslaught, retreating steadily before the pounding breakers riding in on a twelve-foot tide driven by hurricane force winds. Then, when they had cut through these and into the valleys, it had been the secondary dunes which had marched in to do battle. Under most conditions they would have been victors. But not this time. The raging, rampaging sea had continued to rise until it had swept across the dunes and had cleaved temporary inlets between them, and had then pushed the sand fanlike into the marshes, bays and harbors.

At Coast Guard Beach, the bathhouse was demolished while the parking lot was undercut and chopped to pieces. Meanwhile, cottages along the Spit were washed away. The Outermost House, which had been built by Henry Beston in the late nineteen twenties and had been lived in by him for a year, was swept into Nauset Marsh where it broke apart and passed into history. The literary landmark had been given to the Massachusetts Audubon Society which had moved it several times back from its original location as the waters of the Atlantic inched relentlessly closer. But this time the ocean would not be denied and proved once again, to the dismay of many, that along the shore there is no permanence.

For permanence is a relative term and it applies only to that generation currently using it. We look back upon the slaughter of the passenger pigeon, the heath hen, the great auk and almost surely the eskimo curlew with some regret, but mostly indifference. All of these paid the price for our callous selfishness—extinction. Their value to us as a food supply led to their outrageous destruction because the satisfying of our taste buds was more important than their immortality.

Today, the futures of the Ipswich sparrow, the bald eagle, the peregrine falcon and the Least Tern are in jeopardy, but for different reasons. Human encroachment and pesticides are their enemies, but the warnings go unheeded. For as always happens, we forget the fallen and give little thought to those which are endangered. And perhaps, unfortunately, this is the way it is meant to be. Some species pass into extinction, but we must remember that they were products of interbreeding. And as eons slip by, new species appear to take their place. They adapt to their present environment and their numbers fluctuate along with nature's fluctuations. Their lives ebb and flow like the tides, and their so-called permanence is in reality a transitory condition like changing cloud formations. Their lives, like ours, are as ephemeral as the early morning mist rising from the upland ponds in early spring, as tenuous as the alewife fry moving back to the sea in midsummer, and as final as the flying insects being chased by swallows across the summer marsh.

And so it is with the Cape as it is with all coastal areas. They do not have the same appearance today as they had yesterday, and

The Blizzard of 1978

they will not appear tomorrow like they do today. We make the mistake of assuming that any change will be a permanent one when in reality this is not so. We make the mistake of assuming that coastal changes which hurt our lifestyle are for the worst when many times they are not. One only has to watch the determined march of the scalloped dunes into the beech forest; the creation of the barrier beaches from the glacial till of the scarps; the endless shifting of the dunes; the ever changing position of the inlets and harbors. For when nature destroys, it also creates. And given time, it will overwhelm the hand of man. Human lifetimes are too short to measure the effects of either, but what belongs to the sea, the sea will recover; what belongs to the wind will surrender to its will; and what belongs to the land will be reclaimed.

When Tara and Timbre returned to the Spit, it bore no resemblance to what they had left the previous fall. In the middle of the first week in May they flew in from the south, skimming across the flattened dunes, last year's failures forgotten while optimism coursed through their essence, strengthened by the simultaneous swelling of their gonads. Two tiny bits of life they were, their breeding plumage in full glory, bright yellow, black-tipped bills opening wide as their mating calls rattled happily above the unbroken, persistent roaring of the foaming breakers. For seven days they reconnoitered the Spit, searching vainly for a suitable breeding site. But the barrier beach was bare, swept clean of man's efforts, the sands of the once sixteen-foot-high dunes pushing grotesquely into the marsh like cancerous fingers. Finally, they settled onto a gravelly area, behind jumbled outcroppings of broken tarmac and bordering the easterly edge of Nauset Marsh. No sooner were they settled there when signs were posted warning wanderers to keep away from the nesting area. A few days later they were joined by two dozen more Least Terns and the determined colony launched into the business of breeding, while Common Terns began their courtship actions a hundred yards further south.

The terns adapted quickly to their new nesting site. Can we say as much for ourselves? Do we forget that the land is under constant change? Do we forget that an ecosystem is in an everlasting state of flux? The complex web of interdependent lives moves through a maze of chance and transformation and is affected by a dynamism of natural events and man-made forces. The tern, within finite limits, accepts the necessity of having to adapt. They take their chances with their natural enemies. They take their chances with their fluctuating food supply. They take their chances with the calamities of nature, the natural disasters, what we sometimes call "acts of God," and they lead their fragile lives under these conditions with a naive yet eloquent innocence.

But if lower forms of life (as we know them) are expected to adapt and take their chances, then why not we, also? In the ultimate scheme of events, is not the disappearance of an island formerly used by the terns for nesting as meaningful as the destruction of a barrier beach where summer cottages once served the pleasures of vacationers? Should we not be as concerned with the erosion of a beach cliff where bank swallows previously nested as we are with the disappearnce of a beach front parking lot which is important to the economy of a town? Is it not time to learn that what we have is only on temporary loan to us? When a barrier beach is taken away, its sands travel elsewhere to begin again. The act of destruction in one location leads to construction in another. And when waterfront property which was once a salt marsh is erased into oblivion by a massive ocean storm, future generations will see it as it once was, an expanse of luxuriant, gleaming green, producing estuarine nourishment for migrating shorebirds and nesting seabirds. Should we not accept the sea's retributions as lower forms of life do? If we want to intrude upon the sea's domain, shouldn't we learn to accept the consequences? And did we really never know, or have we merely forgotten, that life must end in order for life to continue.

Tara and Timbre, like the others, tried gallantly to bring forth new young, but their attempts were fruitless. Sightseers came to view the destruction of Coast Guard Beach, and although their intent was not to disturb the Least Terns as they nested in the well-defined colony, their constant presence at its periphery was a continuing upsetting distraction. The terns spent more time in the air warning away the curious than they did on the nest, and their attack rattles in concert with their bold dive-bombing runs ricocheted across the barren barrier beach. On a few occasions, unrestrained dogs ran through the colony, crushing a few eggs, but the most serious damage occurred when red foxes began a nightly foraging in mid-June. They came from behind the salt marsh where their numbers had been increasing steadily for a few years, and the efforts of National Seashore rangers to keep them away were futile. By the first of July, the colony had been abandoned and the Leasts had wandered away to other areas.

Tara and Timbre drifted south to North Beach, vague thoughts probing the possibility of nesting there. Unfortunately, a spinoff colony of herring gulls from Monomoy had settled in the area, and another tern nesting site disappeared. A day later at Harding's Beach, they sensed the presence of great horned owls when they discovered the remains of decapitated Least Terns in the now deserted colony. Then at Craigville, they made one final attempt at renesting but abandoned the eggs when heavy earth-moving equipment moved in and began draining and filling the marsh as a site for a beachside condominium.

By the spring of nineteen hundred and seventy-nine the end

was rapidly approaching for the Least Terns. Poor chick production was causing their numbers to decrease rapidly and scarcely five hundred pair returned to the Cape. The nesting sites of all four species were being swiftly destroyed or overrun. The Arctics were gone and the Commons and Roseates were losing ground steadily. Only seven areas were available for the Leasts, the primary one being at Nauset Heights.

The Spit that year was deserted of terns. Tire tracks of beach vehicles wove deep ruts behind the secondary dunes. Along the ocean side of the barrier beach, surfcasters chased their dreams in the twilight, while behind them motorbikes whined or growled, depending on their horsepower, and weaved sinuous trails between the dunes and along the hardpacked foreshore.

Tara and Timbre returned to their Spit and found it barren. Bewildered, they flew in vain across the dunes, searching for their dreams, longing for their passion, pleading desperately for what was theirs. Within the limit of their feeble intellect, they tried to understand why. Where were the others? Why were they not surrounded by thousands of their peers? Where was that welcome, noisy, agitated, chattering, restless mass of feathery life which they longed for and which was so necessary for the continuation of the species? At Nauset Heights. That's where they were. And reluctantly they circled the Spit one final time, crossed over the inlet and joined up with the colony there. Their optimism, although commendable, was short-lived.

Half of the Least Terns returning to the Cape had chosen Nauset Heights. In recent years, it and the West Dennis colony had been the most productive. But not this year. For the past few years the red fox population on Cape Cod had been making a slow but steady recovery after being almost eliminated by mange disease. Now, beyond the upper limits of the marsh in the greening meadows, fox dens were appearing on the gently rolling hillsides. They were well hidden beneath thickening scrub growth which yielded gradually to a pioneer community of scrub pine, red cedar and locust tree saplings whose initial efforts to reestablish forestland would be be successful before being supplanted by an eventual hardwood forest.

Their choice of habitat was excellent. About the time their pups were whelped, the meadow and marsh were full of moles, shrews, mice and cottontails. In addition, the bushes would soon fill with berries which would add variety to their diet. And now the terns were back, along with their eggs and chicks. If the terns had only their natural enemies to contend with, the two species could have existed together. But with the overwhelming pressures placed upon them by man's ever-increasing population and his continuing encroachment upon their nesting sites, the terns' demise was imminent

The handsome reddish-brown animals with their ash-gray flanks and white-tipped, bushy tails followed their instincts. Their nightly forays into the colony reduced drastically the number of eggs and kept the terns from incubating those which were not eaten. Finally, the unending harassment proved too much and the colony dispersed to try elsewhere.

Tara and Timbre were driven northward. In desperation, they joined up with a small colony at Marconi Beach and produced three eggs which eighteen days later yielded two live chicks. The third suffered a torturous death when ants entered the pipped shell before the chick could crack it open. The fate of the other two was not much better. The food supply along the Outer Beach was poor that year. The two parents searched frantically to find enough for them, but their efforts were futile. The chicks slowly regressed in weight, then died of starvation.

The mourning parents remained in the colony for a few more days, bewildered and uncomprehending. Then, when an unexpected southeaster drove the Atlantic waters into the colony and swept it clean, they headed southwest across the bay. They found the colony at Old Harbor Creek in Sandwich abandoned. Increased development of nearby marinas in combination with a swelling population of herring gulls was the reason. A new landfill dump had been constructed a half mile away, just what the scavenging gulls needed, and the terns surrendered to their domination.

Once again, Tara and Timbre began their southward migration alone. It was not until they met other migrants along the Delaware coast that their remorse began fading. And when they overtook a family of five near the Outer Banks and saw the parents struggling to feed their chicks, they volunteered their help and temporarily adopted the frailer one, feeding it until it was as plump as the others and had regained its strength. The little group stayed together for the remainder of the migration, providing mutual aid, satisfying their flocking instinct, and enjoying a brisk and vibrant sociability which was so desperately needed.

Nauset Spit

CHAPTER VIII

Conditions were no better in nineteen hundred and eighty. The population of the Cape and Islands was increasing at a much faster rate than anticipated. The winter population was almost two hundred thousand, while on any given day in summer, more than five hundred thousand tourists were enjoying the pleasures of the sandy peninsula.

Tara and Timbre dropped down onto the Spit on May fifth. It was deserted. Beyond a narrow channel flowing into the marsh on a rising tide, a hundred pair of Common Terns were roosting on the upper beach, while further back in the mixed flora of beach grass, dusty miller and salt spray rose, a few pair of Roseate Terns were beginning to court. Tara and Timbre stayed in the area for a few days, hazy memories forming from four years before when they had reared their two chicks. Then, when they saw the courtship actions of their larger cousins, they decided to search for others of their own kind.

Their track was south. Nauset Heights was deserted now, as were North Beach, Tern Island and the other islands of Pleasant Bay. Monomoy, which had been cleaved in two by the Great February Storm of nineteen hundred and seventy-eight, was saturated with herring gulls, black-backed gulls and laughing gulls. But not a tern was seen. Along the twisting southern shore from Harding's Beach to West Dennis Beach, the surf whispered fluidly against the fragile headland. They dropped down repeatedly to feed in the glimmering green shallows and endangered estuaries, looking up from time to time, hoping to see others with bright yellow, black-tipped beaks like theirs.

Finally, at West Dennis Beach, they found them. One hundred pairs were nesting in a roped off area behind a low line of grassy dunes which sloped into a gravelly section bordered on the north by a tarmac roadway. Beyond the road was a salt marsh ripening in the spring sun. But if one looked closely, the marsh could be seen shrinking in size as its northern edge was being slowly and painfully filled for home construction.

Tara and Timbre settled into the business of nesting, confident that this was their year. And it was—for six weeks. The two terns let their love flow again like it had four years before. He hovered around her protectively after she had laid the three eggs, and together they placed bits of shell and pieces of decaying seaweed around them in the shallow nest. As the summer solstice neared, the days warmed rapidly and he became aware of her reluctance to leave the nest. So he did what he did best. He fished. As did the others. From dawn to dusk the males could be seen fishing beyond the breakers. Their sleek silver-backed bodies skimmed daringly over the blue-green water, yellow beaks pointed downward as they hovered patiently, waiting for the tiny killifish to approach the surface. Mostly, they would dip quickly and skim the surface skillfully, then rise proudly with the fish in their bills. But sometimes they would strike into the water and live up to their nickname, "the Little Strikers," going completely under before turning upward and breaking through the surface, their "ki-ki-ki" calls ringing across the sands like a miniature anvil chorus. The chicks hatched on the fourth of July, a week after the others, and Tara and Timbre exhausted themselves as they struggled to keep the downy young well-fed. It was worth it, though, and in the stillness of the evening they would caress each other's necks lovingly as they roosted by the nest, their three chicks sleeping contentedly with full stomachs.

The chicks grew rapidly. The colony was well-posted and also well-patrolled by concerned and worried natives of the region. Paradoxically, the colony was located on a small, sandy plain of a busy public beach. Through the years, the colony had prospered each summer together with a steadily growing human population. But the past few years had seen a change. Increasing beach traffic on the ocean side of the dunes along with a greater number of motor vehicles on the paved road to the north ultimately proved too much for the terns to cope with. For these reasons an unfortunate cycle occurred. Tern production reached such a low level that the population of the colony could not be stabilized, and each year the number of returning Least Terns was less than the year before.

Then one evening in early August, just before the fledgling time, the final, tragic blow fell. A midsummer heat wave had poured in over the Cape the day before. The south shore was hot and humid. As dusk deepened into darkness, vacationers still walked the beach, reluctant to return to their motels and cottages. In the northwest sky, heat lightning flickered faintly in the distance. As was usual at this time of night, the terns were restless, waiting nervously for the night to quiet down. It did—gradually. By midnight the beach was empty except for a few surfcasters and some young people roasting marshmallows over a small fire of driftwood. Occasionally, a motorcycle whined along the beach in the intertidal zone, or an automobile followed its headlights along the paved road behind the beach.

Then it happened. They had been drinking beer at a favorite watering-hole on Route 28. As their beer consumption increased, so did the intensity of their friendly argument over who had the faster car. Egged on by their companions, they agreed to a drag race behind the dunes of West Dennis Beach. Twenty minutes later, they were side by side, revving up their throbbing engines which protested noisily in the moonless night. Then they were off, building up speed as they hurtled down the half-mile straightaway.

Tara and Timbre awakened first, apprehensive at the familiar sound. Then the others followed suit. As the roaring sounds came closer, the terns began fluttering about a bit, concerned for the safety of their chicks. Then, seconds later, panic began sweeping through the colony, the chicks lying frozen by an unknown fear as stark as the approaching headlights. Seconds later, the two vehicles were nearing the colony side by side. Then without warning the driver of the car furthest from the colony lost control and veered into the other car. A moment later, both cars plowed into the colony, scattering wildly those adults and chicks that were not smashed to death by the spinning wheels. Timbre escaped unharmed, as did Tara when the rear tire of one car scraped her left wing as she scampered to safety. Tragically, their three chicks died wretchedly beneath the tires of the rampaging vehicles.

For two days, Tara and Timbre hovered about their broken bodies, poking at them gently, trying to coax them to stand and live again. The following day, members of the local bird club moved into the colony, clearing it of the dead birds. Tara and Timbre watched from a distance, calling sadly back and forth. Then, in the early afternoon, they deserted the colony, as did the other terns. They were, however, the only ones that flew northward.

They followed Bass River until they reached its headwaters at Follins Pond. After crossing Route 6A, they picked up the beginning of Chase Garden Creek and followed its twisting northwest course until it emptied into the Bass Hole estuary. They paused here in midafternoon, feeding on schools of small minnows in shallow puddles left by the ebbing tide. An hour later, as the shadow of the narrow footbridge leading to Gray's Beach began lengthening across the quiet marsh, they floated easily above the long-deserted colony, then flew westward across the bay towards Sandy Neck.

An hour later they landed on a deserted stretch of beach a few miles east of Scorton Harbor. The nesting site was empty except for a few broken eggs and a decaying body of a near-fledgling. They fluttered about nervously, looking beyond the upper limits of the beach and across the marsh to a stand of mixed oak and pine trees covering a broad, low hill. As the sun dipped lower in the western sky, an occasional awkward-appearing bird flew out from the trees and soared heavily over the marsh. Their backs were black, as were their caps, and their short, thick-necked bodies were carried on gray wings from which dangled short yellow legs. Their underparts were completely white from their bills to their tails.

One look was all Tara and Timbre needed to understand. They were black-crowned night herons, and their predation of the colony was what had caused its demise. Their presence ended any thoughts of renesting that they may have had. Besides, the days were becoming shorter now and the flow of reproductive hormones was beginning to ebb, while at the same time Arcas began nudging them southward.

In nineteen hundred and eighty-one, Tara and Timbre were one of only twenty pairs of Least Terns returning to the Cape. As they fanned out across the peninsula, arriving at different times in different places, three timeless but conflicting instincts drove them onward. The urge to reproduce, coupled with the flocking instinct and the urge to return to their primary breeding site, left them in an instinctive chaos. All three could not longer be satisfied simultaneously. Confused and tormented by these conflicting instincts, their breeding attempts ended in failure, and when the season ended they had no further interest in returning.

Two chicks had died on Noman's Land when a dummy bomb dropped from a naval airplane had fallen on them. At Wing's Island in Brewster, abnormally high tides had washed away eggs almost ready for hatching. A few others had even tried nesting on Tern Island, but the presence of herring gulls had been too distracting for them. At Marconi Beach vehicles had blundered into the small colony, while at Nashawena red foxes had gobbled up the freshly laid eggs. At Sandy Neck the nests had been run over by motorcyclists, and on a remote stretch of private beach near Nobscusset, a pair of free-running dogs had caused the terns to desert their eggs. Meanwhile, at Gray's Beach a beachcomber had stepped on a solitary egg, never realizing it, and wondered angrily why those two screaming birds kept attacking her.

As for Tara and Timbre, as usual they had returned to the Spit again, finding it infested by humans and their vehicles. A week later, they had tried nesting on Corn Hill near an overturned dory, but had given up when attacked by a great horned owl. Tara had recognized that faint vibration in her ears from years before, and without hesitation she had pushed Timbre under the dory and then had gotten under it herself just before the hungry predator had landed.

Completely unnerved, they had flown away the next day, scouting potential sites, but being endlessly disappointed as they moved steadily southward. Finally, they had attempted one more time at Kalmus Beach near Hyannisport. But it was not to be. A week following egg-laying, the eggs had been run over by a motorcycle.

Completely disheartened, they had returned to the Spit at

Nauset. It was too late for them to breed again, and in that langorous interval of time before Arcas had begun urging them southward again, they had dallied at the inlet, feeding leisurely and enjoying the presence of each other's company. It was at that time that Tara's destiny had begun to change.

As fewer and fewer Least Terns had returned to the Cape each year, and as their reproductive struggles had yielded fewer and fewer chicks, their plight had become widely publicized across the hooked peninsula. But some lessons are learned slowly, the arousal of an intense indignation takes time, and definitive action requires courage. But help was coming. Perhaps it was too late to save the Little Striker, but hopefully there would be enough time to save the Common and Roseate Tern, and if miracles do really happen, then perhaps the Least and Arctic Tern could be resurrected also.

And so a rising storm of public outcry began rumbling across the Cape. Not like a sudden summer thunderstorm which strikes unexpectedly, shakes a wispy fist, then fades quickly away. No, this outrage was conceived deep within the conscience of a few valiant ones, and resembled the embryonic, circling trade winds of the Atlantic Ocean which sometimes gives birth to tropical hurricanes. And like the hurricanes which gain their strength and energy from the warm waters of the sea, this storm drew its invincibility from a moral public indignation. And like the hurricanes which sometimes storm across Cape Cod, the call to save the Least Tern gained strength slowly, and when its great force finally arrived, its power could not be overcome. But this would not happen for another year—and it would be something that Tara would never know. In the meantime, she did not like what she saw. It was Timbre.

For over five years he had been her champion. And she remembered. She remembered their first season together and the joy they had had in raising their two chicks. And although it is said by some that she had little memory (this conclusion was drawn from the very latest scientific data) it is not yet within our power to know how her memory processes differ from ours, and how they are capable of reaching into the past more vividly than ours do.

She remembered the five springs they had raced the sun northward, and how he had led the way, providing a cushion of air for her to ride on. She recalled the countless storms which forced them to land on choppy seas, and the encouragement he would call to her in shrill "ki-ki-ki's" when she knew fear.

Often she would recollect with heavy heart their many breeding failures, and how he had always been there to ease her melancholy and resurrect her spirits. And memories of how he had kept her stuffed with fish and shrimp when she was sitting on the eggs came drifting back through the mists of time like phantomlike visions.

She had fond remembrances of the many times when they had flown together and he had led her across the summer dunes glimmering brightly in the heat of the hot July sun. He had called out sharply to her when he had dipped one wing earthward, but at the same time angling upward as he powered his body up and over the scarp. How many times had they flown wing tip to wing tip out across the Eastham kames until they had found that swirling thermal which had propelled them upward like autumn leaves in a miniature whirlwind.

She savored reminiscing about these flights because it was in the air over the Great Outer Beach that her roots were. And they were deep like the beach grass anchoring the fragile dunes of the Spit. Often she would remember the ultimate joy they had shared, the way they had circled upward, climbing through the misty clouds with him leading the way, the two of them reaching outward for that sublime sensation which can only be known by the buoyancy of extended wings lifting upward through sun-drenched air.

Now, as the season drew near its ending, her thoughts traveled back through time and she remembered how he had loved her. He had been devoted to her, that she knew. From the innermost recesses of her complex mind, she cherished those times he had given courage to her when late spring storms had scoured the Spit with screaming, wind-driven sand and howling winds. And she would be eternally grateful for the many times he had awakened her in time to see a blazing sun lift boldly out of the Atlantic Ocean.

She had not forgotten the colonies they had been part of, that seemingly confused mass of complaining, squabbling, boisterous life which required so many parts in order to exist as a whole. How indelibly had been impressd upon her memory the innumerable times when she and Timbre had felt that sudden restlessness surge throughout the colony. Then, as if their minds and bodies had fused into one (and who knows, perhaps they had), the colony would rise as a unit, and the sky would fill with a disturbed and circling cloud of gray which would sweep low across the foaming sea before returning in a clamoring, raucous-calling flood tide of tumultuous and enthusiastic life.

When she saw the southward migrating shore birds descend upon her sandy plain in July and August and watch over their inexperienced young with anxious eyes, she would gaze at them with a thoughtful longing and wonder what had become of her two offspring. And from these thoughts would flow the questions that she and Timbre had asked many times but had never been answered. What was happening? Where were the others?

So these thoughts were in her mind as she watched Timbre from a distance. He was getting old and they both knew it. The autumn of his years was at hand and she found herself wondering how much more time they would have together. In mid-August, when Arcas began its six month sweep from north to south, he lingered, reluctant to begin their southward migration. She waited patiently, bringing food to him often, speaking to him encouragingly, each day urging him imperceptibly further south. Their autumn molt was at its midpoint, and for a week it mirrored the mood of the weather, gray, cold, subdued and colorless.

They spent the cool evenings roosting on secluded beaches, waiting patiently for clearing skies. They were unencumbered by fledglings, of course, but this tragic result was not as devastating as it had been in past years because now it allowed them more time for each other. One evening shortly after Labor Day they were roosting quietly near a piece of driftwood the size of a telephone pole, on the lower eastern shore of Monomoy. In the east, a huge marigold moon lifted ponderously out of a silent sea whose ebb tide was lapping meekly at the quiet shore. Halfway up in the southern sky, Aquila the eagle was at the midpoint of its journey from east to west.

They spent an intimate hour preening, pausing occasionally to speak in low, gutteral tones. From time to time they preened each other, depositing drops of oil on inaccessible feathers behind the head, then drawing each feather delicately through the beak. They appeared to be slightly restless, but this was not the case. It was simply their manner of communication. Sometimes she would rest her neck against his shoulder, stroking it tenderly. He would accept the caress gratefully, thankful for the years she had been his mate. His favorite response was to bend his head downward and rub the top of it along her lower neck and breast while she cooed softly and patted the top of his head indulgently with her bill.

They continued this interplay awhile longer, then moved further up the beach where mats of gray-green poverty grass had settled resourcefully between clumps of beach grass whose edges and tips were beginning to brown, and stalks of seaside goldenrod whose saffron blossoms gleamed paradoxically like a hopeful spring sun. Suddenly, without any warning, it happened. They had been dozing shoulder to shoulder for about twenty minutes. Then, before they knew what was taking place, a fine mesh net flew out from behind an overturned canoe and trapped them. Overcome with fear, they tried bravely to escape, but could not.

Old Timbre once again took command and calmed her. Quietly, they awaited their fate. Unable to understand what was happening, they huddled close to each other, his reassuring tones soothing her frazzled nerves. A moment later, two human hands held each of them firmly while bright red bands were attached to their left legs. What they didn't know and could never know was that they were the last pair of Least Terns on Cape Cod. They had been watched and followed for a month by Audubon Society members who wanted to document their final days.

Minutes later, they were released, and they retreated quickly to the western part of the island which had been designated a Wilderness Area by Congress in nineteen hundred and seventy. Its ability to support migrating and nesting birds, unimpeded by the distractions of human encroachment, was a welcome reward for those responsible for its salvation.

They spent two more days on the island before starting south. They flew at a leisurely pace, allowing the year's harvest of late migrating juvenals to overtake and flow past them. She waited patiently for him when he was forced often to stop and rest.

It took them six weeks to reach Aruba and when they did, he was exhausted. But the winter tranquility rejuvenated him and they settled into a quiet period when the aches and pains, the weariness, and the onward march of his old age was halted temporarily by the warm climate. She was with him always, making sure he ate well, and foregoing those times when she wanted to fly daringly the way they did when he was younger.

In late winter when their prenuptial molt was completed, she knew instinctively that there would be no breeding for them this year. She couldn't know, of course, that his testes had lost their virility and were unable to respond as they had in the past. But she did see the change in his appearance from former springs. His beak and legs were no longer as bright yellow as hers, but rather were lusterless, as was his cap which was a dull black, almost dark gray. Overall, the grays, blacks and whites of his wings, tail and underparts had lost their sharpness while his voice was no longer as vibrant as it once had been.

They left Aruba on schedule in the spring, but their arrival at the Spit was three weeks late. He was unable to attain the speed of his former years and he was forced to stop more frequently to rest. He was lucky that there were uncharted islands between Aruba and Haiti, islands which buccaneers had visited in the seventeen hundreds, islands which now supported descendants of wild goats they had left there, islands which now were visited only rarely by a few fishermen. They island-hopped northwesterly across the Caribbean until they reached the Florida coast. She stayed with him faithfully. His chest and shoulder muscles tired quickly now, so she flew in front of him throughout the entire journey, creating a cushion of air which was easier for him to fly through. She maintained a continual song of chatter, encouraging him, understanding his silence, knowing what he was going through and how he was concentrating solely on bringing his wings down and forward, up and back, down and forward, up and back . . .

Each day when they halted, she would fish for him while he

rested. Then for a short time they would fish together, fleetingly recapturing the old times, calling back and forth with familiar "ki-ki-ki" sounds. They settled down to roost each evening before sundown, then waited patiently for darkness and the gradual appearance of Arcas and Polaris. Intimately, they would communicate in ways unknown to man, knowing that each day they were falling further behind schedule. No longer did they race the sun northward. By the time they reached the Spit, the Commons and Roseates were already present, although their numbers had been reduced drastically.

It would be a confusing, tragic season for her, this year of nineteen hundred and eighty-two. The desire to reproduce would burn as passionately as it had in prior years, but after two weeks of posturing before him, she realized that he was unable to respond, and she forced herself to be content to fly with him as they passed sand eels or shrimp back and forth.

As they did so, they sensed a change in their Spit. Something had taken place that they could never understand. No longer were motor vehicles or pedestrians allowed where terns formerly nested. For a period of five years, these former breeding sites would return to the terns. All hope had been lost for the Least and Arctic Tern, but it was thought by many that there was still time to save the Common and Roseate Terns. Fences had been erected to seal off these barrier beaches and this had caused much grumbling by many. But the laws and ordinances were being strictly enforced. It was being said by those who should know that if the terns had only to contend with winged predators, then they should be able to make a substantial recovery.

In the meantime, when they watched the meager colonies of Common and Roseates begin their renewal, Tara and Timbre could only wonder—where were the others? But they would never know that they were the last pair of Least Terns on the Cape. And they would never know that their final days were being documented by man with a fervor which was as enthusiastic as it was hopeless.

As soon as they appeared over the Spit, with their bright red leg bands contrasting vividly against its spring colors, the word went out across the country, and within days environmentalists, ornithologists and tern-watchers descended upon the Cape to observe and film what they hoped would be a successful breeding season. But their hopes would soon be dashed and their fears realized. What they were about to see was the demise of a poignant relationship as death gradually crept into and finally embraced one of them.

As spring gave way to summer, he was flying less and less. He knew something was wrong with him. He was always tired. He had to force himself to eat. When he did fly, his chest and shoulder muscles tired quickly and his lungs filled with pain when he took deep breaths. His vision was not as good as it once was and often, when they were flying, the earth and water would begin spinning slowly. It was only when she called sharply to him that he would realize it was he who was rolling, and with great effort he would extend his wings and follow her clumsily back to the Spit.

Time passed slowly and in these final days the warm, sandy beach belonged only to them. He regressed gradually more each day and was satisfied to make only the short flight to the inlet where she fished for him faithfully. She was at his side the greater part of the day, leaving only to feed and to take two 10-minute flights, one in the morning and the other thirty minutes before sunset. It was during these times that she would do her agonizing, and would temporarily rid herself of those angry frustrations which would build up within her.

First she would beat her wings strongly, taking deep bites out of the summer air as she climbed for altitude, wishing that they could have had one more chance together. Then, as she slipped into a rising thermal and rode upward in slow, spiraling circles, she would remember the frustrations they had shared. Gradually, as she surveyed the curving, emerald-green sickle with its tawny-colored edges, these memories would fade away and would be replaced by those of the happy times they had shared in fall, winter and early spring. For a short time she would glide effortlessly, looking down upon either the calm waters of the bay or the more restless fluidity of the awesome Atlantic. Then she would return to reality and drift earthward in a lazy, floating glide, landing close by him as she shouted her familiar call.

Each time he answered her, his call was weaker. One day he refused to fly to the inlet and she knew the end was near. During these final days she never left his side. She spoke to him in whispery murmurs, consoling him, knowing he was in pain. Gradually his legs weakened and he could no longer rise. His eyes closed for longer periods of time and he could only answer the solicitous comforting caresses of her bill by nodding his head in short, almost quivering strokes.

The end came one morning shortly after a sunrise which he never saw. He was lying on his side, looking at her through heavy-lidded eyes, each breath more shallow than the one before. He knew what was happening and he hated leaving her. She had been a magnificent partner, he thought, and she had attained the exquisite beauty of a mature female. In these final moments when he felt the chill of death seeping into his body, he struggled desperately to gain the strength needed for a final farewell. She was bent down close to him, pecking at him gently, comforting clucks emanating from her throat. Her heart was breaking. She hated seeing him this way, remembering the strong, virile Timbre of years ago, he who had been her valiant consort. Yet she had always known that it must end sometime. With a last effort, his deep brown eyes cleared for a moment, he raised his head off the sand and his beak touched hers. Then, and although it was weak, he uttered the familiar mating call to her one final time. When he returned his head to the sand, his eyes closed and he lay still.

She knew he was gone. What she didn't know was that they were not alone. One hundred yards away, a ranger had watched the scene through long-range binoculars. He continued watching for more than an hour. During this time Tara stayed close to Timbre's body, at times uttering muffled sounds of grief as she stroked him devotedly with her bill. A few times she hopped away, fluttering her wings at him, as if urging him to fly with her, knowing that his lifeless form would never fly again.

The ranger lowered his glasses and headed in their direction. Halfway there he had to detour around a small group of Common Terns whose reaction was predictable. He was fortunate to be wearing his wide-brimmed hat, and for two or three minutes he was kept busy ducking away from their determined attacks; twice he felt their excrement splattering on it.

It was their harsh "kearrs" which drew Tara's attention away from Timbre. At first she watched the ranger curiously, but as the distance between them narrowed she began moving about nervously. She didn't know what to do. The high tide had been coming farther up the beach each day as the moon approached full, and she knew that if the noon tide did not claim his body, the midnight tide would. She was willing to accept this, the ultimate law of nature. What she could not accept was a predator dismembering him and leaving only feathers. And this was a predator. Yet as he came closer, she relaxed somewhat. He was talking to her in hushed tones, moving slowly but steadily toward her. When he was six feet from Timbre's body, he stopped for a moment and they eyed each other. She had backed away a few feet. He crouched low, then crawled slowly forward on his hands and knees, still speaking softly in muted tones. She didn't move. Somehow she sensed she need not know fear. And when he picked up Timbre's body and held it gently in his hand, she sensed from the look of anguish on his bearded face, and the tone of heartache in his voice, that all would be well with Timbre. The ranger extended his arm in her direction, expressing silently his sorrow. Then he turned away, taking Timbre with him.

She never moved. And her eyes never left him until he disappeared out of sight behind the curve of the beach. For a few moments she poked around the spot where Timbre had spent his final hours. Then, as a blazing sun began making its power known along the barrier beach, she realized that she hadn't eaten for over two days. A moment later she was in the air, heading for the inlet.

CHAPTER IX

Now she was alone. And for the first time since her third year, she knew loneliness. It was not easy to forget Timbre. From late July until well into September she was constantly reminded of him. In the latter days of the month, the midsummer flood of migrating shorebirds began with a trickle of semipalmated plovers. Sea rocket was blossoming in the sand, their small lavender-colored flowers appearing cross-like against their thick, fleshy stems. Meanwhile, flea-bane was painting the borders of the ponds with the same hue, while in the woodlands wintergreen was pushing forth their small, urn-shaped flowers.

The plovers came surging in from the north in large flocks, resting on the upper beach at night, then at dawn fanning out across the tidal creeks, mudflats and beaches to feed. The small shorebird is brown above and white below in all seasons, and at this time of year they still sported black-tipped orange bills and bright orange legs, and their dark breast bands which gave them the name "ring-neck" had not yet begun fading to their winter color of light brown. Tara watched them with a pensive sadness as they ran along the beach in short, quick bursts, then cocked their heads to one side momentarily before picking up a small morsel of food.

In early August, before the Cape took on that slightly used look, least sandpipers, semipalmated sandpipers and sanderlings appeared, flooding the coastal zone with fragmented flocks as they paused leisurely in their journey from northern Canada and Greenland to the southern coast of the United States. Tara watched them come and go, listening to the high-pitched beeps of the leasts, the lower-pitched calls of the semipalmateds, and the sharp, distinctive flight clicks of the sanderlings. All were mottled gray above with white underparts, but the smaller leasts had yellow legs while the legs of the other two were black. And when the three species scampered along the edge of the surf as they fed at the wave-washed shore, the sanderlings could be easily identified by their larger size. It was when Tara looked upon this scene that she remembered when she had had other Least Terns for companions—and Timbre.

A few weeks later she mingled with some Commons and Roseates that were leaving their nesting sites and beginning to drift southward. A few days later they were at Monomoy, where they lingered for two weeks. Occasionally she would remember the year before, when the red bands were placed on their legs, and she would poke at hers fitfully.

Migrating shorebirds continued to arrive and feed along the western marshy shore of the island. Tara watched them come and go with a passive indifference. Only when she saw mated pairs did she look a little longer. And she tried not to notice the Commons and Roseates that had fledglings to feed. But this was impossible. Shortly before Labor Day, she decided to move on. A few days later she was at Great Gull Island. The last of the Leasts were ready to leave and paid little attention to her arrival. But she was assimilated into the group without question, and she migrated and stayed with them all through winter.

When the spring of nineteen eighty-three arrived, Tara faced troubling conflicts. She migrated north with the other Leasts, acutely aware that she had no mate. This was disturbing. She continued to remember the years she had shared with Timbre and how resourceful he had been. Then she recalled their final year together and how their roles had changed. Now, as breeding time neared, it was even more difficult for her to accept the loss of Timbre. Yet she was as unable to repress her biological clock, her hormones, her genes, as was any other form of life. It was so dictated that she must reproduce. And as her ovary enlarged, and as Arcas tugged her northward, one burning desire coursed through her being like a swollen, overflowing stream in spring. She must breed. But where?

She lingered at Great Gull Island for a few days, sexual excitement racing through her veins as she watched the pre-copulatory interplay taking place among the Leasts. There were hundreds of them present, along with just as many Commons and Roseates. As their mating actions took on a more serious tone, the struggle between her instincts became more intense. Often she would be sought after by males trying to attract her attention by offering minnows to her. And many times she would play the game, enjoying the pure exhilaration of having someone to fly with. Other times, when she was flying across the beach, she would hear the authoratative calls of the males winging upward at her from their staked out territories. And sometimes she would follow these calls down, her breeding instincts bursting forth like spring flowers, and for a short time she would flirt with them. But each time they would peck at her she would break off the sport and fly away, leaving a confused male behind. But not as confused as she. The flocking instinct was strong and her desire to reproduce was peaking. But this place was not where she should be. She should be further east and north, at the Spit. And each night at eight o'clock, Arcas told her so.

Eventually she became more aloof from the flock, roosting alone each evening, visions of the Spit growing stronger in her memory, and watching Arcas warily as he stared unapprovingly at her. A day later she surrendered to the instinct pulling at her, and she began the final leg of her journey to the Spit.

Now she was the only Least Tern on the Cape. The Commons and Roseates had returned earlier and were back in greater numbers than the year before. She spent a few days satisfying her flocking instinct with the Commons and waiting patiently for the arrival of more Leasts. Each day the desire to breed burned with a greater intensity, and each day her frustrations continued to grow. There were some generic actions she went through which burst out of her like water surging from a broken dam. For two weeks she could be seen bowing before her invisible suitor and twirling counterclockwise, her snow-white breast making shallow scrapes in the sand. Finally, she tired of this and mingled with the other terns, flying, fishing and roosting with them. It was when they began their egg-laying that she decided to search for other Leasts.

She spent the better part of a month looking for them. She would never know what a stir she caused. Her arrival had been awaited hopefully by many, and those birders who did see her were elated and optimistic that she would be joined by a male. Their wishes went unrealized—as did hers. She was seen from Provincetown to Sandy Neck to West Dennis Beach to Monomoy as hundreds listened to her worrisome calls rattling across the quiet barrier beaches.

Thoroughly discouraged, she returned to the Spit. Many of the Common and Roseate eggs had hatched, and her larger cousins were flitting about, their agitated babbling reflecting the typical activity of the colony. She landed at the periphery and watched the scene. Most chicks were less than a week old, their fluffy bodies covered with gray-brown down. Many were tumbling happily in the rippling surf, while the more timid ones remained closer to the nest. All were calling incessantly for food and the adult males were either flying to and fro from the inlet or fishing out beyond the breakers. Behind the beach, in the hollows between the low-rising dunes, Roseate chicks were still in their nests, watched carefully by their parents.

Tara observed the activity with a passive interest. Terns would arrive with tiny fish in their bills, trying to locate their nests. Simultaneously, brooding females would scan the sky, calling upward with soft twittering sounds, chicks screaming constantly, males stealing food from other males, squabbling breaking out over territorial intrusions, then ending just as abruptly.

Then Tara noticed something unusual. Fifteen feet away, a Common Tern was sitting on her nest. She was twisting her neck in all directions, calling periodically in an almost imploring tone. From beneath her white-feathered breast, two tiny heads poked out, their bills gaping, hungry peeping sounds emanating feebly from their throats. They were ignored.

Tara cocked her head to one side. She fluttered closer, her instincts in confused disarray. How she wanted so much to be a part of this. She hopped closer. The Common Tern caught her movement from the corner of her eye. She looked at Tara suspiciously for a moment, then turned away. What neither of them knew was that her mate was gone, having died for some unknown reason while fishing beyond the shoal waters of Nauset Inlet.

Tara would never understand why she did it. Somehow she knew there would be no breeding for her this year. Yet there were other instincts which needed satisfying, instincts which could not be ignored. The instinct to be needed, to be wanted, to be productive came bursting forth like the tiny lavender-colored flowers of the blossoming beach pea. An instant later she was gone, heading for the inlet, not understanding what was spurring her. Once there, she hovered briefly over a tranquil creek until she spotted the minnow, then struck without hesitation. A moment later, she began the return flight to the beach, flinging water from her wings as she increased her speed. Twice she had to warn away would-be thieves with her angry cry.

For three days she worked diligently to bring food to the nest. The Common Tern accepted the food for her chicks without hesitation. Each time Tara returned, the grateful mother greeted her with a hearty "kearr." At first the Common would not leave the nest, not even to feed, and Tara was also kept busy feeding her. Each evening Tara roosted nearby, looking on thoughtfully and reminiscing about those times so long ago that she had shared with Timbre and their chicks.

Late one afternoon, the Common Tern stepped away from the nest, stretched her wings and looked thoughtfully towards the water. She turned around and stared at Tara briefly before calling a sharp, questing "squewt." Then she flew out to join the other females to bathe. Tara walked to the nest and hesitated. The chicks were sleeping soundly, unaware of the profound accommodation which had just occurred. Memories of her first breeding season formed in Tara's mind as she settled onto the nest. And when she experienced the forgotten tactile sensation of helpless life beneath her folded wings, she recalled that joyful year when she had chicks of her own.

The unusual union lasted throughout the summer. Tara had little time to dwell on the past. Both terns were kept busy and they

Tara

encountered no serious problems in bringing the chicks to the fledgling stage. At migration time they were larger than Tara and the scene appeared almost ridiculous when the smaller tern was seen feeding the larger one.

In late August the four terns migrated together until they reached Florida. Then they parted. The Common Terns' winter home was along the coast of Central America and she and the chicks struck a westward course along the Gulf Coast while Tara continued on to Aruba and Venezuela.

The spring and summer of nineteen hundred and eighty-four had been as lonely for Tara as the winter had been in Venezuela. Her return to Cape Cod had not been as happy as the year before. In addition to feeling the effects of the aging process, she had been unable to find any of her species, and she had been ignored by the breeding Common and Roseate Terns. Once again the barrier beaches had been free of human life, and she had observed enviously the successful nesting season of her larger cousins. Her urge to nest had reached its apex in late May and had then plateaued in June and July. At the approach of August the instinct to breed had ebbed, paralleling the shortening days of summer, and she had begun her migration to Venezuela earlier than usual.

Now, on the northern coast of Venezuela which is also the southern rim of the Caribbean Sea, Tara was ending what would be the final winter of her life. Venezuela sits entirely within the Torrid Zone, its southern tip located just one degree above the equator, and its northern coast twelve degrees further north. Because her winter home is so close to the equator, the seasons do not vary much in temperature. The winters, however, which last from May to November, are hot, humid and wet because torrential rains are driven across the llanos on southerly winds. Then, during the summer months from November to April, the cool, dry northeasterly trade winds arrive and the heavy rainfall diminishes dramatically.

So, this was where Tara and Timbre had recuperated from the rigorous nesting seasons on Cape Cod. This was where time had helped heal the scars of heartbreaking failures. This was where they had grown plump from feeding in the estuaries of nameless streams which trickle anonymously into the warm tropical waters of what was once the infamous Spanish Main.

She had always enjoyed this interlude. The Paraguana Peninsula had been a part of her winter home for as long as she could remember. She had been forced, however, to become acclimated to the huge oil refineries at Cardon and Amuay. But as she had grown older she had spent more time on the island of Aruba to the north, and on the narrow fringe of Venezuela on the Guajira Peninsula. Here the coast curves southeast and forms a sandy shore between the Gulf of Venezuela and Lake Maracaibo.

She was unable to recall when Lake Maracaibo and its adjacent lowlands had not been studded with hundreds of oil derricks. She was, of course, unable to understand the significance of these derricks, just as she was unable to comprehend the presence of the huge oil refinery on the island of Aruba. But she had tolerated all of this with indifference and had accepted the accompanying natural environment with relish.

And so, it was more to her nature to be attracted to the marshy mangrove swamps which swept away from the shores of Lake Maracaibo. Here, instead of oil derricks, were short, squat, sturdily growing mangrove trees, their roots anchored firmly beneath the flowing tides while their branches gave birth to the rich, lush fruit.

Tara had spent many of her waking hours flying over the western and eastern spurs of the Andes mountains. She had not ventured above three thousand feet, however, preferring rather to explore the coastal zone between the Caribbean Sea and the mountain range. It was on these steep lower slopes, the tierra caliente or the hot land, as it was called, that much of the Venezuelan tropical fruit, sugar cane, cacao, coconuts and rice were grown.

She had not yet accepted the loss of Timbre. Not that she was yet ready to breed. That hoped for episode was more than two months away. But deep within her subconscious she knew something was wrong. She should not be alone. She should have a partner to migrate with. The frustration of not having one for two years still lingered. She was remembering this while she dozed fitfully on the lee side of a forgotten dory which had been tied to the rotting stump of a once tall palm tree.

Forty minutes earlier she had been feeding fifty yards off the coast of the thirty-five-mile-long channel which separates the Gulf of Venezuela from Lake Maracaibo. It had been a busy and hectic feeding hour. A large school of mackerel had chased thousands of minnows into warm, shallow waters and she had enjoyed the brisk sociability of the other terns while she had eaten. Most of them had been Common and Least Terns. Still, she had felt like an outcast because she had known that none of the Leasts would be returning to the Cape. In addition, she had been poignantly aware of the first signs of a fresh awareness among them. Mating pairs of prior years were becoming attentive to each other when they flew together across the barren dunes, or fished side by side in the crystal-blue waters.

An iguana rustled in the sand a few feet away, then climbed onto a large charcoal-colored rock to sun. Then a pair of Arctic Terns came gliding in from the southeast and circled overhead. One landed on the stern of the dory while the other flew along the waterline. They were larger than Tara, perhaps by six or seven inches. Their upper parts were a pale blue-gray while their bills were carmine red and their feet and legs the color of coral. They were stopping briefly to feed and rest on their journey north from the Antarctic to the Arctic where they would nest and raise their young. Their continual chattering was annoying Tara while her glance at the iguana was not friendly. When a flock of Common Terns flew out over the water, then returned to continue their perpetual bickering, she had had enough.

She stood up and ruffled her feathers. Then, as was her habit, she gave a gentle poke at the red band around her left leg. She knew that it should not be there, and she did not like it. But somehow she sensed that it had a protective significance and therefore she accepted it. She gave it another poke with her bill while a barely audible grating sound of reluctant surrender arose from her throat.

She stepped into the bright sunlight and hesitated. A moment later she pushed firmly against the white-colored sand and lifted her buoyant body into the air. She gained altitude rapidly, using the outer primary feathers of her wings like tiny propellors. She raised her wings rhythmically above her body until the tips of these primary feathers almost touched. When she thrust her wings downward with her strong chest muscles, the primaries were pitched in such a way that they bit deeply into the air as they swung through a vigorous half circle. It was this superbly orchestrated up and down cadence which pushed her through the hot, dry air.

A few minutes later she was soaring easily over the channel. She was riding a thermal which was rising briskly from the broad, sandy beach below, and she was drifting upward in tight, lazy circles. When she reached an altitude of twenty-five hundred feet, she slipped away from the updraft and lowered her left wing, angling her right wing upward at the same time. In this way she entered a shallow glide which gradually reduced her altitude to two thousand feet. She feathered the air deftly with her primaries, rocking back and forth slightly from side to side. Her reactions to the slight but never-ending variations in the air currents were automatic, her forked tail maintaining her in level flight, one side or the other constantly dipping or rising to give her the necessarry stability. She tilted her head earthward and to the left. Down below, a short, weather-beaten tugboat was towing a heavily-laden oil barge upcurrent to the entrance of the Gulf. She stared at it thoughtfully for a long time in silent recognition but was still, as she always had been, uncomprehending.

Abruptly, she made a right turn and increased her speed. For over three hours she followed the coast eastward towards Coro. The northeasterly trade wind was blowing from her port quarter at an angle of forty-five degrees and was cool and dry. She knew that the direction of the wind would change soon when it would sweep out of the east, southeast and south and bring the winter rains with it.

She breathed in deeply and felt a temporary quickening of her spirits. The airstream was flowing across the upper surface of her wing at a greater speed than it did across the lower surface, and the lifting effect floated her upward while she drifted aimlessly along the coast toward Coro. A Common Tern glided upward past her starboard quarter and uttered a quick call. She ignored the casual greeting and looked earthward. The stretch of seacoast from the Maracaibo channel to Coro was desolate, the naked land being bleak and deserted while the hot, sandy dunes wove a formidable barrier between the warm waters of the Caribbean and the San Luis mountain range.

The distance from the Maracaibo Channel to Coro is well over a hundred miles and it was a long flight for her. As she neared Coro the dune country was desertlike, with little vegetation. Not far away, however, long rows of breakers poured endlessly across submerged reefs, their whitecaps foaming with a deep tinge of gold in the late afternoon sun. A few miles up the coast she could see clearly the beaches of Coro trimmed boldly with coconut palm trees.

She knew this would be her final winter. The coming spring would be her thirteenth and she was tired. Not only the physical weariness of old age, it being more difficult for her now to perform the dainty flying acrobatics which she once had executed with ease, her weariness was rather from struggling with the frustrations and anxieties of the past nine nesting seasons. The instinct came filtering back through the mistiness of time and she knew she would try once more.

She flew easily like a dainty wisp of dandelion fluff floating haphazardly across a thick green lawn in spring. A sudden gust of wind almost flipped her over, but she fought it neatly by automatically tightening her chest muscles and pulling in her wings slightly. Her eyes narrowed at the landscape below. She had come close enough to the western perimeter of Coro.

She turned northward and felt the wind change direction against her body. Now it blew steadily from her starboard quarter at an angle of ninety degrees. Her course was a few degrees west of north but she maintained a northerly heading to counteract the trade wind. Her landfall was the western shore of Aruba seventy-five miles away, and although she did not realize it, her final spring migration had begun.

There were reasons for this. Her prenuptial molt, under the influence of her gonadal hormones, was finished. In addition, she had completed the accumulation of fat which was essential for a successful migration. She had also become acutely aware of the imperceptible progression of the sun along the eastern and western horizons as it rose and set seconds earlier and later each day. This northerly progression went unnoticed by human senses. But Tara knew. She had to know, for she set her course by the sun when she migrated.

A few hours later she crossed over the northern coast of the Paraguana Peninsula, and a few moments later Aruba edged over the horizon. There was a very good reason why Tara began her migration from the western tip of Aruba. Give or take a few degrees, its longitude was the same as Nauset Spit on Cape Cod, seventy degrees west. It had been bred into her genetic memory, her celestial clock, that her guide was Polaris, the North Star. She knew if she kept Polaris directly ahead, she would reach Cape Cod. Once in the area, she would find her way by visually identifying landmarks which had been pointed out to her by her parents. But there was one final key which got her moving, and that was Ursa Minor, the Little Dipper, known in Greek mythology as Arcas, the Little Bear.

That evening, after the huge orange-yellow sun had settled into the Caribbean Sea, and after its purple-reddish reflection off the thin, scattered mares' tails had finally disappeared, and after hundreds of discordant-sounding terns around her had at last settled down, Tara stared at Arcas standing twelve degrees above the horizon and understood. Tomorrow she would leave her winter quarters . . . and not return.

CHAPTER X

Because of her age, Tara's final migration took two weeks longer than usual. She could not fly the long distances that she once did, and she didn't try. She conserved her strength as she made her way up the coast, her final stops being at Great Gull Island for two days, and Block Island for one. Instinctively she knew her ultimate destiny lay at the Spit, but she did touch down on those resting spots where for hundreds of years her forebears had paused.

When she reached Nobska Light she was seen at once and recognized by her bright red leg band, and the call went out. By the time of her arrival at the Spit a hundred eyes were trained on her, and a hearty cheer resounded when her yellow legs and yellow, black-tipped bill were seen flashing brightly in solitary splendor among the larger Commons and Roseates.

Her commanding breeding plumage deceptively camouflaged her years. She was tired and the initial hints of her mortality were beginning with chest pains following long, strenuous flights, But in spite of this, within her ovary two ova were gradually approaching maturation as once again her desire to breed blazed with a renewed vigor.

She spent a week recovering her strength, feeding by herself at the inlet but flocking with the Roseates and Commons that were at the midpoint of their nesting season. This was their third one since the breeding sites had been protected by law, and all across the Cape their recovery was increasing. These larger cousins of Tara were nesting on the marsh side of the Spit about a quarter of a mile south of the chain link fence which sealed off the Spit from Coast Guard Beach.

At the beginning of the second week in June Tara drifted away from them, her instinct drawing her a half mile further south to the vicinity of her primary nesting area. It had changed, of course, and no longer resembled that place where her first brood of chicks had been born, and where Timbre had died. But she could tell when she was where she should be, and she spent another week either flying above the site, waiting anxiously for the arrival of her suitor, or pretending he was already there and had called her down. Then generic actions would take command and once again she would pivot counterclockwise in the sand, making shallow scrapes and bowing demurely before her imaginary partner.

TERNS NESTING
THESE ENDANGERED BIRDS ARE HARMED
BY ANY DISTURBANCE
Keep Below High Water Mark At All Times
DO NOT ENTER
AREA BOUNDED BY SIGNS - PLEASE NO DOGS
Posted by Mass. Audubon Society Per Order Board of Selectmen

As summer began she was becoming discouraged. Common and Roseate chicks were hatching in increasing numbers, and in her territory piping plovers and willets were raising chicks back in the low, undulating hills of sand where the Spit was struggling heroically to regain some semblance of its former configuration before the Great February Storm of nineteen hundred and seventy-eight.

When she saw the small, sand-colored plovers with their bright yellow legs and feet and dark neck bands, and heard their piping, organ-like calls drift back and forth to one another, she remembered her final summer as a pre-adult when she had flocked with that small group at Wellfleet. But when she saw the barely visible balls of fluff which were their chicks scampering in the sparse clumps of marram, she was once again reminded of the years when she and Timbre had struggled fruitlessly to raise their chicks.

The pair of willets usually nested in Nova Scotia, but a May northeaster had forced them to take shelter on the lee side of the Spit, and they had decided to stay. Now, the marbled-brown, foot-long shorebirds were busy raising their two chicks and they found the tidal creeks of Nauset Marsh to be a rich source of food for the family.

Tara, torn and tormented by the continual frustration of failure, decided to leave her primary nesting site. Her instinct told her that if the male was not here, he must be somewhere else. She had no desire to change a ritual which had been bred into her species for centuries. Nature dictated that when unmated she must fly over territories held by males who must call her down. She forgot about Timbre. She forgot about earlier nesting seasons. Her ovary was pouring reproductive hormones into her bloodstream at such a quickening rate that she was becoming maddened by the lack of a suitor.

She left the Spit and followed the coast northward as she had the year before. She was frantic now, knowing that this was her last chance. She drove relentlessly onward, tortured by the conflicting urgent instinct to mate, yet living with the pernicious specter of old age and impending death. She was in constant discomfort when she flew, tiring quickly, not reacting to the capricious wind currents as she used to in her younger years.

It took her a week to scan the Cape. If she had not tired so quickly, if her chest had not hurt so much, if her shoulder, wing and wrist muscles had not ached so much, it would not have been so difficult. But she did not have the stamina she once had. She had to stop and rest often, and it took her longer to feed. She was not as quick as she once was and it was becoming more difficult for her to hover and strike with the sureness that she once had. Because of this she was being drawn more to the tidal creeks where at low tide she could find shrimp and minnows.

Once again her pilgrimage took her along the Outer Beach to Provincetown, where she turned the corner and followed the bay coast to the Audubon Sanctuary at Wellfleet. Along the way she saw numerous colonies of Commons and Roseates nesting in unaccustomed tranquility and raising near-fledglings in numbers not seen in many years. But neither did she see the mate she had to find nor did she hear his call. She rested for a day in the thick marsh of the sanctuary. These last few days of June were burning hot, presaging what the summer was to be and equaling the intensity of her mating urge. She allowed herself this one day to enjoy the crisp, cool shelter of the tall cord grass. Then she was off again. She must find him.

She continued searching from First Encounter Beach to Sandy Neck, then southward to West Dennis Beach and easterly to Harding's Beach and finally Monomoy. It was hopeless. As she struggled home over North Beach towards the inlet, she was a vanquished piece of ebbing life. She was exhausted. She had lost all hope. She would never find him. The season's end was fast approaching, and even if she did find him they would be hard pressed to get the chicks ready in time for a successful migration.

It was late afternoon when she reached the inlet, but the sun still hung high in the sky, scorching the land mercilessly and forcing the Commons and Roseates on the Spit and at Nauset Heights to keep their late-born chicks covered with their wings. The tide was halfway towards the ebb, flowing briskly towards the sea, sweeping a convoy of clean cut catamarans with it. She stood wearily at the edge of a shallow stream waiting patiently. After a few moments a school of minnows began flowing past and she fed hungrily, swallowing each minnow head first. As she satisfied her hunger she felt better, looking up from time to time and watching the Commons and Roseates as they fished out beyond the shoals.

Then, without warning, it happened. She could not believe what she saw, and for a brief moment she was stunned. She had resigned herself to being alone forever and an instant later he was standing three feet away from her on the other side of the shallow stream. His name was Timor.

He was a handsome Least Tern. He was the same size as Tara, in his first breeding season, and his engorged testes were pouring reproductive hormones into his bloodstream at an ever-increasing rate. He was excited. He was energetic. He was potent. His breeding plumage was sharp and vibrant. His movements were quick and sure. His voice rang with confidence. He would be her consort. He would be her savior.

He had been born in nineteen hundred and eighty-three at Cape Fear, had wintered on Aruba with his parents and had returned to the colony as a non-breeder the following spring. But

Tara

something had happened to him during his second winter in Venezuela, something which he would never be capable of understanding. A mutation had occurred mysteriously in the gene which controlled his migratory instinct. In late winter when the first visions of his breeding home had been forming in his tiny brain, they were not those of Cape Fear. These visions were of a land eight degrees further north and five degrees further east. They were of a narrow spit of land protecting a great marsh and there was an inlet leading into this marsh. These strange visions, however, had created conflicts in Timor. When he had taken the usual route northward and had reached Cape Fear, he had remembered this pleasant, quiet, gravelly beach where he had been born, and he had been drawn earthward.

But Timor no longer belonged at Cape Fear, and somehow he sensed this. He had watched the other males stake out their territories, and call to the females and court them with squirming shrimp. He had watched their rituals of courtship. He had even attempted to become part of the colony. His generic actions were strong enough. He was young. He was ready. Yet, the final component was missing. This was not where he should be. Arcas was not where it should be. Its position in the sky did not correspond with the new imprinted location on his mutated gene. The Little Bear should be higher in the sky and more to the west.

Timor began drifting northward, at first a few miles each day, searching instinctively for that narrow sandy Spit, the inlet, the marsh, where the position of Arcas would match perfectly with that molecular transfiguration which had miraculously taken place in the gene. He was completely overpowered by this strange turn of events. Nothing else would matter until he had found the Spit. And from deep within his psyche his instinct told him that that was where he would find her.

It had taken him two months to reach the Spit. Along the way he had visited at Montauk, Great Gull Island, Nashawena, South Beach, West Dennis Beach, Monomoy, Tern Island and Nauset Heights. It had been over Nauset Heights that he had seen his destination. He had been flying at an altitude of six thousand feet, which was a bit more than his usual height. But it had been an unusually warm day and the higher he flew, the cooler it was. Then he had seen the final piece of the enigma and his gene had been satisfied.

He had reached the Spit the day before Tara's return and had claimed his territory. Twice he had reconnoitered the area, pausing to feed at the inlet before returning to begin his vigil. It was when she had dropped down at the inlet that he had seen her. He had decided to wait no longer and had flown down to greet her.

Now, Tara stared at him unbelievingly. And when his harsh

"ki-ki-ki" burst heartily from his throat she jumped back, almost falling. An instant later his head bobbed rapidly up and down in the stream. Quicky he had a minnow in his beak and he fluttered across the stream and offered it to her. Startled, she accepted it while he quickly caught one for himself. Then he flew north towards the Spit, calling over his shoulder for her to follow.

When she appeared over the territory he called her down, and she alighted near the spot where the old weatherbeaten log had once rested. He approached her with a strutting swagger, and when he pecked her lightly on her shoulder and she bowed her head, their courtship began, and they both knew that it must be brief. Time was growing short. Still, the ritual must be observed. They were an odd pair, this old and tired female and the young virgin male bursting with a boundless energy which was astounding. It did not take him long to realize that she was old, and he adjusted to this without hesitation. In the meantime he was prepared to follow her lead in the ritual of courtship.

She led him through it patiently, becoming exasperated at him only at its climax when twice he mounted her the wrong way and stared at her upraised tail with a bewildered look. Twice she shook him off, scolding him at the same time. On the next try his generic actions prevailed and their union was consummated.

Somehow, and though it had been only for a brief time, he had rejuvenated her. Once the eggs had been laid, however, she was content to brood them for days at a time, allowing him to feed her. Only three times did she leave the nest to refresh herself, and each time it had been more difficult for her to do so. He sensed the developing tragedy, knowing that once the chicks had hatched there would be much work for him.

That happy event occurred late in July, and already the days were becoming shorter. As August made its appearance summer continued hot and dry, the unwelcome drought draining the precious moisture from the land. They were fortunate that the inlet was close by and also well stocked. Timor labored tirelessly, and because he was young and strong he had little trouble keeping the chicks and Tara well-fed. It was an easy time for her. She remained near the nest, watching with a relaxed eye her chicks scampering about the territory, somehow knowing intuitively that there was little to fear. She would tolerate the heat with little complaint, waiting patiently until the growing chicks sought the cooling shelter of her outstretched wings. In the early evening Timor would spell her faithfully and she would walk slowly down to the surf where she could bathe sedately, marveling at his youthful exuberance and remembering those days when she possessed an identical passion.

By mid-August the chicks were halfway towards being fledged. During this time Tara had much time to reflect. She had not forgot-

Timor feeding a chick

ten Timbre. Yet she had no regrets about her relationship with Timor. Both had profited from it. But even though he was her mate and the father of her chicks, she had trouble adjusting to his actions. He was full of a boundless energy, but clumsy and awkward, sometimes dropping food before reaching the nest or bringing sand eels too large for the chicks to eat. Then she would scold him angrily and he would back away, surprised and flabbergasted at her tone. But soon he would be off again, flying to and from the inlet, fighting off those Commons and Roseates which at times would attempt to steal the fish or shrimp from his bill.

Each evening he would roost by her side and she would sleep deeply, knowing that he would only half sleep, instinctively maintaining a wary vigilance. It was at these times when he comforted her, knowing that her time was ending. A few days before Labor Day the chicks were fledged. She was able to fly only short distances with them, the pains in her chest becoming more severe each time that she flew. Instead, she was satisfied to watch Timor as he gave them their flying lessons over the late-summer-tinged barrier beach.

Two weeks later they had completed their autumn molt. The mantles of Tara and Timor had darkened considerably, while their bills and legs had turned a drab dusky yellow. The two fledglings in their first winter plumage resembled the two adults and could be identified only by the expert. There had been many of those around during the unusually hot summer, and Tara and Timor would never know how much joy and excitement they had brought to those who originally thought that they were seeing the last of the Cape Cod Least Tern. Now, as the days of September wore on, they were about to witness the final act.

As Arcas inched imperceptibly onward in its counterclockwise journey around Polaris, Timor became more and more restless and worried. It was time to be moving south. He was working as hard as he could to fatten up the fledglings, at the same time encouraging them to fish for themselves. Sadly, he knew Tara would not be with them. She could only watch them now, suffering her own agony. Arcas influenced her no more. The parade of years had dimmed his power over her, as they both knew it would.

Timor had continued to bring fish to her, but not as frequently as he once did. He did not have the time. Each day Arcas was pulling at him with greater strength, and a few times he drifted south with the fledglings to Pleasant Bay. But he kept returning, calling to her anxiously, instinctively trying to urge her southward, yet understanding her refusal. She stayed close to the inlet, knowing that the feeding was much easier for her there. She was flying very little, her strength becoming weaker with each passing day.

On the evening of the autumnal equinox they gathered together one last time as a family. The two parents roosted together while the fledglings watched from a discreet distance. A nearly full moon rose steadily over the marsh and bathed the silent barrier beach in the reflected light from the sun. Arcas twinkled brightly in the northern sky. A southerly breeze whispered through the marsh, the tall cord grass bowing gracefully before it. The tide was rising, the tidal creeks filling rapidly as the flood tide spread across the timeless marsh.

Tara and Timor roosted quietly, facing in opposite directions, their necks criss-crossed like feathery scissors. In ways unintelligible to other species they communicated on and off throughout the night, pausing sometimes to doze fitfully or sleep soundly for brief periods. She did most of the speaking while he listened patiently, telling him that he must go. He must see that the fledglings reach Aruba safely. He must see that they return to the Spit in the spring. A few times he tried to protest but she shushed him lovingly, caressing his neck with her own, marveling at the strength in his young muscles, thankful for what he had given her. She looked over at their two offspring for a moment and her eyes misted. Then she continued telling him that he had to go, for he was the salvation of their destiny. She had done all that she could do. It was up to him now. If he failed, then all of the agony, the frustration, the misery which she had endured would have been in vain. She did not tell him about Timbre. For there would never be another Timbre. She touched his neck softly with her bill. There would never be another Timor, either. She told him that he would find another mate. Arcas would see to that. And he must bring this mate to the Spit. He must breed again. Their children must breed. Their children's children must breed. He must lead them back from the brink.

For a few moments she was silent, waiting for her words to take effect. He said little, but what he said was profound. Why him? He had had so little time to play, so little time to smell the flowers. So little time to be free and enjoy life. And so little time to love. His eyes were cold and angry and resentful.

The words came easily for her. Because you were chosen, as I was chosen. And you must not fail. For we must survive here. We must. And some day you will be free, as I will be soon. But we will meet again. We all will meet again. And then we will say to each other that we did what we had to do. We did what we were chosen to do. And it was worth it.

He was awake at the first light of dawn. He raised his wings high above his head and stretched. It would be another hot day. The thin low clouds on the horizon first took on a pale-lavender hue, then slowly turned the color of deep rose. As the dawn deepened, the Spit, inlet and marsh came alive with shorebirds. Piping plovers, black-bellied plovers and ruddy turnstones fed along the edge of the surf, each in its own particular way. Within the marsh greater and lesser yellowlegs along with a solitary pair of Hudsonian curlews probed the tidal creeks for crustaceans. Overhead, three pair of Canada geese flew northward on a short flight from Little Pleasant Bay to Provincetown. Two hundred yards out beyond the breakers a pair of black-backed gulls rode impassively on gentle swells. Above them a few mottled-brown yearling herring gulls circled aimlessly, at first sailing downwind on outstretched wings, then turning and stroking their wings forcefully as they labored to regain the lost altitude. Beyond the black-backed gulls a young osprey fished, at first hovering, then striking into the water for its prey. Unexpectedly, a small group of seaside sparrows exploded into view, chirping brightly as they skimmed across the dunes and disappeared into the marsh. Beyond the marsh and high above the rolling kames Timor recognized the tiny speck in the brightening sky as an immature red-tailed hawk out early for its morning exercise.

Timor turned and looked northward when he heard the commotion. A quarter of a mile away and fifty yards out a mixed group of Common and Roseate Terns were moving southward, their loud babbling signaling their pursuit of a school of silversides. Timor called the fledglings and they flew out to join them. As they worked their way southward Tara followed them with tired eyes. Her entire body ached with old age. Yet she stood complacently as she watched her young mate with his endless energy feed the fledglings, at the same time encouraging them to fish for themselves. Periodically he would bring a fish to her and for a short time they would speak in muted tones, either touching bills or nuzzling their necks together. Then, invariably, the fledglings would come soaring in, calling with agitated voices for their parents to feed them.

She kept telling him it was time to go, but for over two hours he kept returning. The beach was warming quickly and as it did it warmed her old bones also, and she felt better. Just before noon they said goodbye, and he and the two fledglings began their southward journey. She stood quietly for over thirty minutes, relieved that the goodbyes had at last been said. Then she heard his call again and looked up. He came gliding in with a silverside in his beak and landed briskly by her side. He was alone, the fledglings circling impatiently a half mile further south.

She did not want the silverside but she forced it down, not wanting to hurt his feelings in these final moments. Their eyes met for too long a period of time and she could see the anguish he was suffering. She spoke to him soothingly when he bent forward and rubbed his head against her breast. You must go now, for the sake of the young ones. Resignedly he raised his head and gazed skyward for a moment. Then he turned and touched her bill with his. He was in the air abruptly, circled once for altitude, then called a final adieu to her. Her return call was weak and quivering, but he heard it. She watched the three of them until they faded from her view.

She felt better now that they were gone. Perhaps it was selfish of her to feel this way, but she had done all that she could do. It was up to Timor now, and she knew that he would not fail. Not Timor. He was too stubborn, too strong, too dedicated. He knew what he had to do.

She felt stronger. The early afternoon was bright and clear and unseasonably warm. She stretched her wings skyward. Perhaps she should get some exercise. Impulsively and without thinking she took two quick steps and was airborne. She struggled for altitude and the Spit grew smaller as she made her way through five hundred feet. It was near the old Coast Guard station that she found what she was looking for. The thermal was not a strong one, but it was enough to give her added buoyancy and she rode it airily, extending her wings as far as she could, exulting as she felt the rising warm air push against her feathery body.

She circled easily, looking across her domain, remembering the seasons she had spent here. Autumn was drifting across the peninsula and the season was new to her. Usually she was gone by this time, but now she had a few brief moments to view the familiar terrain in its unfamiliar foliage. Golden-yellow seaside goldenrod overran the primary dunes while crimson three-leafed poison ivy grew in rambling clumps between beach plum and bayberry bushes which were serving up their berries to those species which needed them for survival. She had a few brief moments to soar across the gold and russet rolling moors and flattened marshes. She had a few brief moments to gaze upon the pitch pine, red cedar and juniper trees which would not drop their leaves but instead would withdraw within themselves while surrendering their once vibrant hues of spring and summer green to those duller shades reserved for winter. She had a few brief moments to contemplate the gold of the birch, the vivid yellow of the red maple, the brilliant ocher of the sassafras, the flaming red-yellow of the oak, the somber bronze of the beech. It was like a multicolored fresco which had been painted just for her. She had one brief moment to watch some migrating monarch butterflies on their long journey to Mexico, their bright orange, black-bordered wings contrasting vividly against the dunes as they flew lightly between stalks of beach grass. Then the pain struck.

It burned deep in her chest and took her breath away. So deep that she lost control and began tumbling earthward. She was frightened. She had to get back to the Spit. She tried extending her wings but it was too painful. She was gasping for breath. The ground was

Nauset Marsh

rushing up at her. She unfolded her wings. Her fall slowed to a clumsy glide and she soared awkwardly across the border of the marsh and Spit, losing altitude rapidly. She had to reach the ocean side but first she had to clear the tops of the low dunes. It would not be easy. An instant later she could see that she would be unable to do it. Not without stroking her wings. Her chest hurt so much. It was becoming more difficult to breathe. What was happening to her? She was going to hit those dunes. Without thinking, she extended her wings and stroked once, twice, three times. The crest of the dunes stopped rushing at her, paused for a moment, then receded away. She cleared the dune by a scant three feet and soared fifteen yards towards the surf. Then she crash-landed not more than ten feet from where she had been born.

She was able to stand just long enough to settle her wings. Then she fell over on her right side. What was wrong with her? Why couldn't she stand? She must be tired. Perhaps if she did not breathe so deeply her chest would not hurt so much. Why had it turned so cold? Where did that thick gray fog come from? Her eyes glazed over. She must rest. Then she would feel better. She closed her eyes for a few minutes. When she opened them the pain was gone. But it was becoming colder. Then she saw the ranger in the growing darkness. Why was he running? The instinct to fly still remained, yet she was unable to move. She could barely see him when he knelt by her side . . . and she would never know that he was crying . . . or why. For a brief instant she could see Arcas, and he was reaching for her. She felt the ranger's fingers close around her tired body and raise her from the beach. She opened her beak to warn him away with her attack rattle. It never came.

Instead, the firmament brightened with a light stronger than she had ever seen, and she felt an unexpected and mysterious breath of life surge through her essence, and she was buoyant again, and she was young again.

Then she heard them. Hundreds and hundreds of thousands of Least Terns were darkening the sky. And they were flying towards her. And they were calling to her. Leading them were her mother and father. And behind them was Timbre. And behind Timbre were the chicks they had lost at Marconi Beach, and the chicks they had lost at West Dennis Beach. They were all there. And they were calling to her. Come, Tara, they were saying. It is time to go. It is time to fly with us. You have done what you were chosen to do. And you have brought us back from the brink.

Seashore Ranger tern watching

EPILOGUE

It is not supposed to rain on Cape Cod in the tourist season. The sun should shine every day. The beaches should be full. Children should be playing on these beaches alongside mothers who should be participating in the ritual of the tan.

But not this day. This dully, dreary day dripped. The rain fell in a slow, steady, persistent drizzle. It puddled on the sidewalks. It etched tiny gullies in the scarp bordering the beach. It dripped endlessly from the gutterless roofs of damp summer cottages. It transformed the dry dirt parking lots of these summer cottages into muddy quagmires.

Furthermore, the rain changed loving families in these cottages into caged, irritable individuals, each trying to break out. The man was one of these individuals. His young, bubbling, attractive wife had become a grumpy, nagging shrew who had insisted on going shopping at the Orleans Plaza. There were few things that the man would not do with his wife. Shopping was one of them. He had left her at the plaza and now he and his six-year-old daughter were driving slowly westward on Route 6A in Brewster. It was still raining and the windshield wipers were swinging cadently back and forth making a faint "thunk" at the top of each stroke. Traffic was heavy. The man was thinking, no one seems to *be* anywhere, everyone seems to be *going* there.

"Where are we going, daddy?"

"Where do you want to go? How about Sealand?"

"We've been there."

"How about the Drummer Boy Museum?"

"We went there last year."

"So we did," the man mumbled.

"What?"

"I said, 'So we did.' " He had raised his voice louder than he had intended and his daughter looked at him apprehensively.

"Sorry about that."

They rode a few more moments in silence. Then a large maroon sign with white lettering appeared on the right side of the road. He pulled into the crushed-stone parking lot and parked between two cars. One was from Virginia, the other from Canada.

"What is this?" the child asked.

"It's the Cape Cod Museum of Natural History."

"What's in there?"

The man thought for a moment, wondering if his daughter would be bored. He changed his mind when he saw a couple leaving the museum with a young boy about the same age as his daughter. The smiling child halted in the steady rain and reached into the paper bag he was carrying. The man caught a quick glimpse of a wildlife coloring book before the boy's mother closed the bag and hustled him into their car.

"I'm not sure. Maybe some animals or birds. And maybe we can find you a coloring book." He felt uneasy. He wondered why he hadn't stopped here before. Perhaps he had never noticed the museum. He could not recall seeing it advertised in the local papers. Perhaps he hadn't been looking for it.

Inside, they wandered through the rooms, stopping briefly in the library to the right before going downstairs. For some time, he studied a geological map of Cape Cod while his daughter was kept busy watching some fish in a large aquarium. Then he carried her for a few moments while they eyed some mounted birds in glass-enclosed cabinets. Each bird was labeled, so it was easy for him to answer her questions.

Upstairs again, they sat and looked through the windows on the north side of the auditorium. Outside, many resident birds were feeding on the scattered seed. The man watched his daughter as much as he watched the birds. Her head moved rapidly from side to side and her eyes flitted quickly back and forth as she followed the darting movements of the winged creatures. They took turns flying out of the surrounding bushes to the feeding stations and moving about on the ground.

After a few moments she became tired of watching, and he lost her momentarily when he became absorbed in observing a gray catbird hopping about on one foot. The other was drawn up tightly against its abdomen. His cursory interest was becoming sympathetic when he noticed his daughter was no longer by his side. Startled, he turned around quickly and gave an inward sigh of relief when he saw her in the gift section of the small museum.

She was staring at some brightly colored science magazines. An elderly museum volunteer watched her carefully. When the man neared his daughter's side, she turned away from the magazines and walked across the corridor to a glass-enclosed case which contained eight mounted sea- and shorebirds. They were gulls and terns except for one in the far corner which was a piping plover.

Two robin-sized birds had caught his daughter's eye. One was pale gray with a black cap, brown eyes and yellow legs. Its bill was also yellow, with a black tip, and it touched the bill of another bird whose mantle was of a darker shade of gray and whose black-tipped bill and legs were of a dusky yellow. Both birds had snow-white underparts and bright red bands encircling their left legs. It was these bands which had drawn his daughter to the case.

"What kind of birds are those, daddy?"

He squinted in the dim light and moved closer to read the label. "They are Least Terns," he said, not knowing what a Least Tern was.

The young child placed her tiny hand in his. "Why do they have those red things on their legs?"

The volunteer worker had been eavesdropping and she felt it was time to join the conversation. She smiled easily at the man. "The Least Tern on the left is a male and died five years ago on Nauset Spit. The one on the right was his mate and she died almost two years ago almost on the same spot." She leaned forward and placed her hand lightly on the child's shoulder. "Both of them had been banded at Monomoy the year before the male died."

The man's frown was a silent question.

The woman smiled again. "I see you are unfamiliar with the Least Tern. Most people are." She thought for a moment before continuing. "Years ago there were tens of thousands of them here. They nested on islands and remote barrier beaches, but the increased tourist traffic pushed them out." She paused for a moment. Then in an afterthought she said, "Among other things." She turned towards the terns, then continued. "This was the only Least Tern seen on the Cape in 1983 and '84. But it returned the following year with another mate and raised two chicks." The woman's face became somber. "But in the fall, when it was time to migrate, she refused to do so and died an hour after the others had left."

"I'm sorry to hear that," the man said.

"You shouldn't be," the woman answered. "An autopsy showed the tern had died of old age. And we think the story will have a happy ending."

The man was surprised at his genuine interest. "Why is that?"

The woman sat down in a nearby chair. "Last year, a pair of Least Terns returned to the Spit and raised two chicks. They were accompanied by two other Least Terns which were just a year old. We think it was the former mate of this one and that he had found another partner. And this year, two nesting pair returned along with two more young ones. Altogether, three chicks were raised and fledged. And they haven't been seen for a week. So we think they have migrated south."

The child looked up at her father. "Daddy, can I have a coloring book and can we go now?"

"Of course," he said absently as he took her hand. He looked at the tern again, then back to the woman. "Wouldn't it be something," he asked, "if we could only know how her life was lived? What her good times were? What her bad times were? She must have been an extremely courageous bird."

The woman gazed solemnly at the two Least Terns. "There are some things that we can never know," she said, ". . . or understand."